LeAnn Rimes

teen country queen

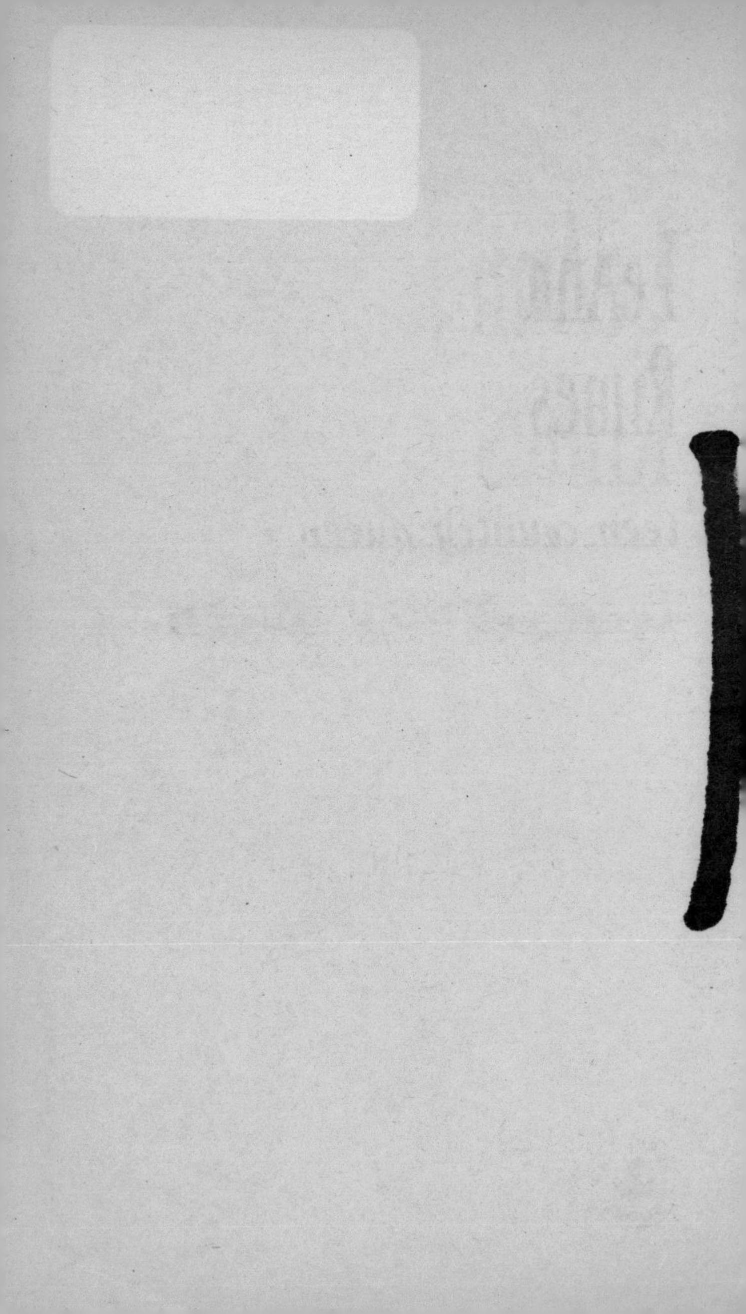

LeAnn Rimes

teen country queen

Grace Catalano

Published by
Bantam Doubleday Dell Books for Young Readers
a division of
Bantam Doubleday Dell Publishing Group, Inc.
1540 Broadway
New York, New York 10036

ISBN: 0-440-22737-2

Printed in the United States of America
May 1997
OPM 10 9 8 7 6 5 4

To Mom, Dad, and Joseph,
for all our travels to Nashville.
The road seems to get shorter
from New York.

Contents

Acknowledgments

The author would like to thank Rose Miele, Sam Alan, and Phil Berry, without whom this book would have been impossible. I appreciate your time, encouragement, and assistance. Thanks also to Grace Palazzo, Ralph J. Miele, Mary Michaels, and Jane Burns.

And special thanks to Beverly Horowitz, Kathy Squires, and everyone who worked on this book at Bantam Doubleday Dell.

1

Country's Teen Queen

It is the morning of June 11, 1996, an unusually cool summer day in Nashville, Tennessee. LeAnn Rimes, teenage singing sensation, is waiting to perform in front of thousands of country fans at the annual weeklong Fan Fair.

Fan Fair, which has been held every year since 1972, is a huge outdoor festival of concerts and autograph sessions on the Tennessee State Fairgrounds.

At just thirteen years old, LeAnn is both excited and anxious. Mike Curb, head of Curb Records, is there to give his new star moral support. Her debut album is still weeks away from release, but her first single, "Blue," has already climbed the charts. Country music fans are buzzing about LeAnn's unbelievable singing range.

It is still early in the morning, but thousands of fans have begun to gather at the show. There is a feeling of mounting excitement in the air, and the people milling about the stage can sense it with every passing moment. Even though other Curb recording artists like Tim McGraw, Jeff Carson, and Sawyer Brown are also performing, it is obvious the audience is there to see "the little girl with the big voice."

A passing cloud drops a light rain, but it doesn't dampen LeAnn's spirits. By the time she is introduced, the sun is shining—and so is LeAnn. She comes out onto the stage smiling and waving and is met with thunderous applause. Her big moment has arrived. The crowd cheers wildly.

As she begins to sing her retro runaway hit, "Blue," LeAnn is thrilled to see and hear members of the audience singing along. Later, she says to her mom, "Can you believe they know my song?"

LeAnn Rimes's dreams came true on that Tuesday morning in June, the day she officially performed her debut single, "Blue," in front of country music enthusiasts and curious industry executives. It seemed as if everyone in Nashville came out to see the hot new star on the country music scene.

After the set, Bob Whittaker, executive producer of the famed Grand Ole Opry, extended his hand to the young singer and introduced himself. "We would like you to appear on the Grand Ole Opry," he said to a surprised and honored LeAnn.

For LeAnn, who began her career by singing on the little Opry circuit in Texas, the moment was extraordinary. Playing the Grand Ole Opry in Nashville was something she had dreamed about all her life. She had never expected to accomplish her goal so soon. She knew it took some artists years before they were invited onto country music's legendary stage. But after hearing her sing "Blue" and watching her work the audience, Bob Whittaker knew that this new star was ready to show her talents on the Grand Ole Opry.

LeAnn Rimes has hit the big time, and success couldn't have come to a more deserving young singer. In less than one year, LeAnn has taken the country music world by storm. Not since onetime teen sensations Brenda Lee, Tanya Tucker, and Marie Osmond dominated the charts has a teenager skyrocketed to fame so quickly.

LeAnn burst onto the music scene not only with the traditional country sound of "Blue," but also with a different, younger, and more energetic sound lacking in country music today. After the super success of Garth Brooks, Billy Ray Cyrus, and Shania Twain in the early 1990s, there was very little excitement left in country music. Until LeAnn came along, few new artists broke free from the sea of newcomers churning out lack-luster pop-style tunes.

LeAnn quickly became country's bright light and a pure breath of fresh air. She has been dubbed Nashville's Teen Phenomenon and Country's New Sensation. She reminds many of the legendary country singer Patsy Cline, especially after it was revealed that the song "Blue" was originally written for Cline forty years ago.

The year 1996 belonged to LeAnn Rimes. Her first major-label album, *Blue*, debuted at number one on the *Billboard* country chart and number three on the pop *Billboard 200* album chart. By the time LeAnn turned fourteen years old on August 28, 1996, she received her first gold record as a birthday present.

LeAnn's success is not limited to the United States. Her album shot to number one in Canada and Australia, making her an international star overnight. LeAnn's debut disc has gone double platinum in Australia, platinum in Canada, and gold in England. LeAnn's first trip overseas was to Australia, where she was named the top-selling female country artist of all time.

Her debut album has sold like hotcakes and secured LeAnn a spot in the country music history books as she continues to break one record after another. Country superstars like Alan Jackson and Reba McEntire haven't been able to beat her on the charts. When Alan's and Reba's albums debuted in early November 1996, they bumped LeAnn to third place on the *Billboard* country album chart. But in just two weeks LeAnn was back to number one and Alan and Reba were at numbers two and three.

By December 1996, LeAnn's number one album was the biggest-selling country disc of the Christmas season. *Blue* was number fourteen on the list of the top twenty pop albums of the year. By the end of the year, *Blue* had sold two million copies and had gone double platinum. At last count, it has sold almost three million copies.

The week of December 16, LeAnn's third single, "One Way Ticket (Because I Can)," hit number one on the *Radio & Records* chart and she became the youngest country singer in history to have a number one song. The record had previously been held by Tanya Tucker, who was also fourteen when her song "What's Your Mama's Name" topped the charts in 1972. When "One Way Ticket" zoomed to the number one spot on the *Billboard* chart, LeAnn became the first young female artist with a number one song and a number one album on the charts at the same time.

LeAnn Rimes seems to have come from out of the blue to set the music world on its ear. In her first year at the top, she has received recognition from practically every music award show, including the Country Music Association Awards and the Grammys, and she won an American Music Award for Best New Country Artist.

LeAnn receives five hundred fan letters a week. Her fans want to know everything about her, especially what she's like offstage. There is definitely more to LeAnn than the girl onstage singing her heart out. At only fourteen, she's already been performing half her life. She's worked long and hard to get where she is today.

What is LeAnn's remarkable appeal? What does she have that sets her apart from the rest? For one thing, she is adored by everyone who meets her. Her outlook on her life and work is always positive. She often uses the adjectives *cool*, *neat*, and *nice*. She is friendly and down-to-earth, a regular teenager who loves to go shopping with friends and has posters of her idols, Bryan White, Billy Dean, and Shania Twain plastered on her bedroom wall.

It's clear that success hasn't affected LeAnn one bit. Her girlish giggle and vivacious personality have established her as the girl next door. LeAnn is honest, independent, original, and fashionable.

There are many sides of LeAnn. She is the pretty teenager who belts out hit after smash hit. She is the young country singer whose dynamic voice baffles the experts and delights audiences. She is the girl whose concert appearances cause excitement everywhere she plays. She is Country Music's Teen Queen, the girl everyone is talking about. She is LeAnn Rimes, and this is her story.

2

A Natural Talent

LeAnn Rimes, born on August 28, 1982, in Jackson, Mississippi, was the miracle baby of Wilbur and Belinda Rimes. The couple were high-school sweethearts who fell in love and married at seventeen. They were eager to begin their lives together and start a family. But they soon learned it wouldn't be as easy as they had planned. Not long after they were married, they were told they couldn't have children. The news was heart-wrenching, but Belinda still cherished the hope that one day she would have a child.

Wilbur and Belinda settled in the small town of Flowood, Mississippi, about ten miles south of Jackson. With a population of only 2,860, Flowood was the epitome of a small town, but the big city of Jackson was not far away. Belinda worked as a receptionist, and Wilbur sold equipment for an oil company. They had everything they wanted except a child.

As the 1970s passed, Belinda and Wilbur saw their dreams of having children crumbling. But Belinda still hoped, and in 1981 she turned to prayer. "Within six weeks," she says, "I was pregnant with LeAnn. Wilbur and I agreed that we would devote our lives to her."

Flowood, Mississippi, was where LeAnn spent the first six years of her life. It was the place that nurtured her zealous determination to become a star and the place where she got her first taste of performing.

From the beginning, LeAnn was independent. She always wanted to keep busy doing new and different things. Her preschool years were filled with gymnastics, tap dance lessons, baseball, and T-ball. But singing was her first and true love.

LeAnn was introduced to music at a young age. Her mother loved to sing, and her father was an amateur guitar player and singer. Belinda sang to baby LeAnn every night and was thrilled when, at eighteen months old, LeAnn joined her in singing "Jesus Loves Me."

LeAnn resembles her mother—she has her features and smile, and she says it's from her mother that she gets her bouncy personality. But LeAnn also has her father's mannerisms. "I think I am a combination of my mother and father," says LeAnn. "The combination worked well in our home. My dad was strict, but not too strict, and my mom was a little more lenient. I think it was a perfect balance. The three of us are very close."

Belinda and Wilbur recognized their young daughter's talent almost immediately. Her father describes her singing as "a gift from God. She came here with it." At two years old, still only a toddler, LeAnn used to sing herself to sleep. Her mother says LeAnn had such a passion for singing it was "like she knew what she came into this world wanting to do."

LeAnn was first influenced by Broadway show tunes and artists like Barbra Streisand and Judy Garland. She would listen to her parents' old records and imitate everything she heard. Her early years were consumed with music. Not only did she sing, she also strummed her father's guitar.

Remembering those days, LeAnn now says, "I could sing better than I could talk. You could understand every word when I was singing. But you couldn't understand what I was saying when I talked."

Wilbur understood that his daughter was a musical natural. Without taking any lessons, she sang on pitch. He taped her voice because he couldn't believe what he was hearing. "When she was only two years old, I'd pick up the guitar and she'd sing along," he says. It became a weekend hobby for Wilbur to set LeAnn up next to his tape recorder. "My dad has tapes of me doing "You Are My Sunshine," "Getting to Know You" (from the Broadway show *The King and I*), and "Have Mercy" by the Judds," she says.

One afternoon, LeAnn listened to her dad trying to yodel on the song "All Around the Water Tank" and showed him the right way to do it.

Growing up in a creative environment definitely had a positive effect on LeAnn. By the age of four, she had started singing for her family and her parents' friends whenever they'd come to visit. It wasn't long before people started to tell the Rimeses they should try to get LeAnn into show business.

Her dance teacher was the first to mention to Wilbur and Belinda that they should consider entering LeAnn in some local talent contests. At four, LeAnn was already projecting not only talent, but also personality and bubbly charm.

But regardless of her boundless energy and interest in performing, the Rimeses weren't sure they wanted LeAnn competing in talent shows just yet. She was only a child, and Belinda thought the work and strain would be too much for her. Belinda didn't want LeAnn to feel discouraged or disappointed if she didn't win.

But they soon realized that LeAnn was feeling

disappointed at not being given the chance to show what she could do onstage. LeAnn wanted to sing more than anything. Belinda and Wilbur decided they would do all they could to get her started.

In 1988, when LeAnn was just six years old, they entered her in a local talent contest. They had never seen her so excited. She practiced "Getting to Know You" for weeks and was ready to perform it at the show.

Her parents brought the budding singer to the competition, but Wilbur decided to leave early. For some reason, he began to doubt that LeAnn would have a chance at winning. He realized that the other children competing were twice her age, and he couldn't imagine the judges voting for his six-year-old.

Even though LeAnn performed "Getting to Know You" perfectly at the talent show, Wilbur thought she just "did okay." He left Belinda and LeAnn at the show and decided to spend the rest of the day hunting in the Mississippi woods. He figured he would know soon enough whether or not LeAnn would win a trophy or go home empty-handed. He was just too nervous to wait around for the results.

Wilbur arrived home at the same time as Belinda and LeAnn. Much to his surprise, his four-foot daughter was carrying the large first-place trophy through the front door. She had swept the local talent show by taking home five awards.

Belinda remembers that her husband was so happy "he just started crying." He would never doubt LeAnn's talents again. "I couldn't believe she won the whole thing," he says. "I haven't been hunting since. And I've never underestimated her again."

That day would be a turning point in the lives of the Rimes family. LeAnn, filled with dreams and confidence, told her parents, "I'm going to be a singer. I'm going to be a big star one day."

Though her parents have been criticized for pushing LeAnn into show business, the truth is that *she* really pushed *them*. "I know all little kids have dreams of what they want to do when they grow up. Mine never changed," she says. "I don't know how I knew what I wanted to do, but I did. My mom and dad have really been supportive of me. I told them what I wanted to do and they just kind of helped me along. I've kind of pushed my parents more than they pushed me. They've never been backstage parents."

LeAnn had been bitten by the performing bug and wouldn't let go of the conviction that she wanted to become a singer. She felt a fire burning in her to succeed at everything she tried. Once she had set a goal, she went after it with a vengeance.

Belinda says of LeAnn, "She was always

strong-willed. She was always this way—straight ahead, focused. When you've got a child like that and you're not like that yourself, it kind of makes you that way. When you've been laid-back and easygoing, you have to roll with the flow and see what happens."

LeAnn's vision of becoming a singing star was never dimmed by the thought that it might be difficult to get ahead in show business. Her parents never scoffed at her dreams and her grand goals. In fact, it was just the opposite.

Soon after the talent show, Wilbur Rimes began looking into places where his young daughter could gain a little experience performing onstage. He was all for the idea of getting LeAnn started singing professionally. He soon became as determined as his daughter to enter the world of show business.

"I knew she was going to be successful in the recording business because somebody would recognize her voice for what it was," he says.

He began by making calls and setting up auditions for LeAnn. The only problem was that there wasn't a lot happening in Mississippi. Wilbur knew that if LeAnn was going to have any kind of chance, the family would have to consider moving. Texas seemed like the place to go.

In Texas there were many avenues open to young performers. Wilbur knew if he was able to get LeAnn into the Texas shows, she'd be making a step in the right direction. But Wilbur still had to be convinced that her love of singing wasn't a passing phase LeAnn was going through.

He took her aside one day and asked her, "Is this really what you want to do?"

LeAnn replied, "Oh, yes, Daddy, it's all I ever want."

With that, Wilbur requested a job transfer to Dallas and sold his truck and hunting dogs to make extra money. The Rimes family was on its way to Texas. Out on the open road, they had a future of uncertainty before them. They had no way of knowing what awaited them or whether LeAnn's dreams would be realized. All they knew was that LeAnn was far too talented not to be given a chance.

"I always knew I could make it if I tried," says LeAnn. "My parents were great in doing everything they could to help me. I had a whole lot of confidence, and I believed I could do it. And if you don't think you can do something, nobody else will."

At the tender age of six, LeAnn Rimes was on her way. Before she knew it, she would be working steadily as a singer.

3

Little Miss Dynamite

In Texas everything seemed to fall into place for LeAnn Rimes. Once the Rimes family arrived in the Lone Star State, they moved into a two-bedroom apartment in Garland, a suburb about fifteen miles north of bustling Dallas. LeAnn was anxious to begin auditioning for shows in the Dallas area, and Wilbur and Belinda started taking her to tryouts.

Looking over the local talent, Wilbur decided there was no reason why LeAnn shouldn't be up on the stage performing. She could sing better than any other child. What did it matter if she was only six years old? She had a burning passion to perform.

"I didn't really set a time line for myself," says

LeAnn. "I really just wanted to accomplish my dream of being something, and I wanted to start early."

The musical world that had influenced the very young LeAnn Rimes was a combination of pop music, show tunes, and old-time country songs. But country music was quickly becoming her favorite. Inside of a year, she stopped singing Barbra Streisand and Judy Garland songs and started performing vintage country numbers.

Her interest in country music began the day she discovered Patsy Cline, the legendary country star of the late 1950s who died in a plane crash in 1963. LeAnn was powerfully influenced by Patsy's voice and music. Patsy Cline was, after all, considered one of the best female country singers of all time and was the first female artist to "cross over" and make hits on the pop charts.

Every female singer who has come along since has undoubtedly been influenced by Cline's vocal styling. Her voice was unique; she sang her songs with strong emotion, pronouncing each word with feeling.

LeAnn's favorite song was Patsy Cline's "Crazy," which had been written by Willie Nelson. It was the song LeAnn told her father she wanted to learn to sing. But Wilbur didn't think LeAnn should sing a song like "Crazy" just yet. He realized his little girl didn't know what the song was about, so he decided to explain the lyrics to her.

"I explained to her that 'Crazy' was about someone getting their heart broken," he says.

LeAnn remembers, "Dad would explain that it was a sad song, and I would sing it that way."

She decided to sing "Crazy" at some of her auditions and decided the song was her lucky charm. In Texas her career as a performer took off. Jobs started pouring in at a furious pace, and life for the Rimes family shifted to the fast track.

For LeAnn's official debut in Dallas, she appeared on a float in a local pageant. As she waved to the people who lined the streets, she attracted a lot of attention. No one believed that such a young child could sing so well. She chose to sing "I Want to Be a Cowboy's Sweetheart," which had been written and recorded by Patsy Montana in 1935. Patsy's song was the first million-selling country record by a female singer. Filled with tricky yodeling, the upbeat song is a true test for a female country singer. At only six, LeAnn mastered the intricate yodeling and performed the crowd-pleaser perfectly. She sang the lively country standard at most of her shows on the Texas stages.

It didn't take long before LeAnn worked her way up to steady spots on local shows. She gained her first exposure on the Dallas–Fort Worth Metroplex Oprys, a group of "little Opry" stages in the adjoining towns Garland, Mesquite, Greenville, and Grapevine. Some have said the Dallas–Fort Worth region has more music than Nashville. The shows held on the Opry stages in the Texas Metroplex usually take place on Saturday afternoons and evenings. With the help of her parents, LeAnn would make the rounds and perform on a few Opry stages every Saturday.

Most children her age would have crumbled under such a demanding schedule. But not LeAnn. Her mother remembers those days vividly, especially how determined her daughter was. "It's just amazing what she has done," says Belinda. "She'd be sleeping in the car as we drove to the next Opry, and then she'd get up on the stage and sing 'Crazy,' and then get right back in the car and go to sleep."

There was little time for rest and practically no time for extracurricular activities. LeAnn discovered that the road to stardom wasn't an overnight trip. It took time and work to prove her talents. Driven by an ever-increasing confidence, she believed that practice would make perfect. She was working hard and paying her dues. Instant success was by no means waiting in the wings.

At the age of six, LeAnn was a bundle of talent all rolled up in a pretty package. She was so good at everything she attempted that her parents decided to take her to an audition for the lead role in the Broadway production of *Annie II*.

The show was the sequel to *Annie*, the phenomenally successful Broadway musical based on the comic strip *Little Orphan Annie*. The original show had been a training ground for future stars like Sarah Jessica Parker and Alyssa Milano.

In 1988 the producers of the original production held a casting call for *Annie II*. A whole new generation of young hopefuls was trying to nab one of the roles. LeAnn tried out for the role of Annie, and her first audition went very well.

In fact, out of the hundreds of little girls trying out for the sought-after part, LeAnn got a callback—an invitation to a second audition. She didn't get her hopes up too high because there was no guarantee that she would win the part.

The other girls trying out were older and had worked in theater. Most of them had résumés that listed many plays and musicals. Even though LeAnn had started out singing songs from Broadway shows, she didn't have any experience with theater yet.

After auditioning for the second time, she got the disappointing news. The casting director explained to her that even though she was terrific, they thought she was too young to carry the show. Another thing that held her back was her Southern accent. The rejection initially upset LeAnn, but it was an experience she is now glad she went through.

"It was difficult when I lost the role," she says.

"But my parents were great. They were really there for me. Now I look back on that time as a learning experience. I think I learned about rejection a lot earlier than other kids who get into this business. You have to deal with the rejection. It's just part of it." To console her, LeAnn's parents bought her a dog she named Sandy—the name of Annie's dog.

The following year, LeAnn made her stage debut and wowed Dallas audiences with her performance as Tiny Tim in a musical production of Charles Dickens's *A Christmas Carol.* LeAnn threw all her emotions into the role and received rave reviews in the local papers.

But while acting and dancing came naturally to LeAnn, music was still the chief passion in her young life. She submerged herself in music so deeply that it began to worry her mother. At times Belinda feared that LeAnn was missing out on a regular childhood. Because she worked so much, she didn't have time to make friends. Belinda was happy when LeAnn started school and began to spend time with children her age.

LeAnn was so friendly that she didn't have any trouble fitting in with the kids in her class. She made some close friends in school and was an excellent student. But her mind was never off music.

She was extremely ambitious and told her parents she wanted to continue singing on weekends. She knew she would have to find time to practice singing *and* do her homework. But that didn't seem to bother her. Schoolwork came as easily to her as music had. Despite her heavy workload, she maintained a straight-A average in all her school subjects. With her ready-for-action attitude and positive thinking, nothing was ever too much for her.

Good things seemed to come her way. When LeAnn was seven, she met Johnnie High, who soon became the most influential man in her early career. He ran the Johnnie High Country Music Revue, the long-running weekend show that had launched the careers of country singers Gary Morris and Linda Davis. Johnnie agreed to have LeAnn audition for him.

"I had auditioned hundreds of kids, but I never heard anyone sing like LeAnn," he says. He remembers being so impressed with LeAnn's rendition of Patsy Cline's "Crazy" that he got goose bumps. He signed her as a regular on his show that same day.

"I never doubted LeAnn for one minute," he says. "She had poise, dedication, and stage presence. She didn't look like a pageant girl. She looked like a country singer, and she just came out and did it. And you know, this success has not changed LeAnn one iota. She still calls me Mr. Johnnie in that sweet little Southern-girl voice."

Though LeAnn was only seven, she quickly became a favorite performer on Johnnie High's weekly show. Dressed in frilly white dresses, she sang classic country songs, surrounded by a band of local Dallas musicians, with her father playing guitar. She built up a following—people came from miles away to hear her sing.

The Johnnie High Country Music Revue, then based in Fort Worth (it has since moved to Arlington), was where LeAnn got the most exposure and the most experience. Johnnie High figured that she did some five hundred concerts with his revue.

"I see these young acts, and they haven't been working a lot," says Johnnie. "But LeAnn has. It's hard to beat getting on a stage every week. She's a girl who knows what she wants."

LeAnn Rimes, even at her young age, stood out. This little girl was dynamite, and she had what it took to become a star. Her outstanding talents were obvious to everyone who saw her.

By now she had become a regional celebrity on the Johnnie High Country Music Revue. Week after week, audiences who came out to hear her sing didn't realize they were helping to make entertainment history.

Johnnie High sees LeAnn's success as something that was meant to happen. "Sometimes someone deserves success and they don't get it," he says. "I was raised on a farm, and we would milk cows at night, and when you woke up in the morning, the cream was at the top. It's kind of that way with LeAnn. The ones that are really great, somehow, some way, it seems to happen to them."

In 1990, LeAnn was chosen to appear on the television show *Star Search*. She felt lucky that she was being given the chance to sing in front of a television audience. *Star Search* had been a staple on the small screen for more than eight years and had given a career boost to many performers. Future country stars like the group Sawyer Brown and Texas honky-tonker Ty Herndon first performed on *Star Search*.

On every show, young actors, dancers, comedians, and singers showcased their talent. The winners, determined by a panel of judges, returned the following week and faced new challengers in their categories.

It wasn't easy to get a spot on *Star Search*. Most young hopefuls who entered were never even chosen to appear on the show. Every year *Star Search* talent coordinators and producers went through thousands of audition tapes. They had a limited number of spots each season and needed to select what they believed was the best young, untapped talent.

When they heard LeAnn sing and found out she was only eight, they decided to sign her to appear on a show during the 1990 season. The producers thought LeAnn was fantastic and way beyond anyone else her age.

On the show LeAnn sang the Marty Robbins song "Don't Worry About Me" and became a two-week champion. Wilbur and Belinda thought *Star Search* was a great experience for LeAnn. She didn't seem a bit nervous, just excited that she was on TV. After getting a taste of performing under the hot lights on the television soundstage, LeAnn was even more sure that she wanted a long career in show business.

Because of her determination, Wilbur Rimes seriously considered quitting his job so that he could manage LeAnn's career full-time. LeAnn had already racked up a long list of credits, and she gave no sign of wanting to stop. A self-described workaholic, she was obviously working toward a full-time career in the music business. She dreamed of becoming famous someday.

Meanwhile, she continued performing in Dallas. She continued to sing every Saturday on the Johnnie High Country Music Revue. She still performed on the little Opry circuit and also sang the national anthem a cappella at Dallas Cowboys games, the Walt Garrison Rodeo, and the National Cutting Horse Championship in Fort Worth.

It was at one of these events that a Fort Worth disc jockey and composer took note of LeAnn Rimes's incredible singing talent. His name was Bill Mack, and he played a crucial role in the next scene of LeAnn's dramatic rise to stardom.

4

The Song That Started It All

The story of how LeAnn got the chance to record the song "Blue" is as legendary as the song itself. Bill Mack, a disc jockey on the Dallas–Fort Worth radio station WBAP-AM, composed the ballad in 1958 for Patsy Cline to record.

"When I heard Patsy sing, I became a big fan," says Bill, who has been in the country music business for forty-two years. "When I wrote 'Blue,' I thought, 'This is Patsy's song.' "

In 1960 Bill was backstage at one of Patsy's shows in San Antonio. He borrowed a guitar from country singer Roger Miller, who was also on the show, and sang "Blue" for Patsy. Her reaction was, "Get that song to me." Bill had a local singer record a demo for him and sent it off to Patsy's record label.

It wound up in the hands of Patsy's husband, Charlie Dick, who agreed it was perfect for his wife's style. But Patsy was killed in 1963 before she had a chance to record it. Bill Mack was devastated by Patsy's death; he decided to put his song away in a drawer because he couldn't imagine anyone else singing it. "In my mind, when Patsy died, so did the song," he says.

As both a disc jockey and a composer, Bill Mack has enjoyed a very successful career. Known as Radio's Midnight Cowboy, he is famous for telling fascinating stories of country stars on his late-night show. He's been a disc jockey at WBAP for more than thirty years and host of the syndicated radio show *Country Crossroads* for more than twenty-five years.

He has worked with legendary figures like Waylon Jennings, Elvis Presley, and Jerry Lee Lewis. Some of his closest friends are George Strait, Reba McEntire, Tanya Tucker, and Loretta Lynn. And he's had his songs recorded by country legends such as Bill Monroe and Conway Twitty. In 1990 George Strait recorded one of Bill Mack's songs, "Drinking Champagne," and took it to number four on *Billboard*'s country charts.

During Bill Mack's long career, it always bothered him that "Blue" was not a hit. Years after

Patsy Cline's death, two artists recorded the song, but it failed to catch the attention Bill had hoped for. Country singer Roy Drusky, a radio favorite throughout the 1960s, recorded "Blue," but it didn't climb the charts. In the late 1980s it was also cut by a Fort Worth singer named Polly Stephens, who did a torchy arrangement to sell at her shows.

Bill felt he'd never found the right singer for "Blue"—until he heard LeAnn Rimes sing "The Star-Spangled Banner." Bill was so blown away by the eleven-year-old's voice that he knew in an instant he had found the singer he'd spent nearly forty years looking for. He didn't care how old she was. He just knew she was the one who had to record "Blue."

"I was knocked out by this young lady's voice," says Bill. "At eleven years old, it was frightening how unbelievably good she was. My song 'Blue' came to mind. It wasn't that LeAnn sounded like Patsy Cline, it was just that I could mentally hear LeAnn singing the song."

As fate would have it, Wilbur Rimes was in the market for new songs. He was planning to produce LeAnn's first album on an independent label. Bill Mack decided to send Wilbur the Polly Stephens version of "Blue" for consideration.

Wilbur remembers playing the song for the first time and putting it on the side. "I almost threw it away," he recalls. He thought it sounded too old for LeAnn; it wasn't the type of song he was looking for.

LeAnn, however, loved it the minute she heard it. "I knew 'Blue' was perfect for me," she says. "But my dad wasn't so sure. I kept bugging him about it. I remember putting the tape in the tape recorder and saying, 'I love that.' "

As she hummed along with the tape, LeAnn got the idea to add what she calls "a yodel thing" to the song. "It didn't have that little yodel in it," she says. "The word *blue* was just sung straight. I added the yodel a few days later. When I sang it for my dad, he said, 'Okay, now we've got to record it.' "

"That's when I fell in love with it," says Wilbur. "LeAnn put that little yodel lick in it and she really transformed it. She made it her own."

Wilbur contacted Bill Mack and told him they wanted to record "Blue" and had worked on a new arrangement. Bill was pleased with LeAnn's rendition of his song. "She did it exactly the way I wanted it done," he says. "Every time I hear it, she sounds better. She positively raises the hair on the back of my neck.

"People call what she does with her voice a yodel," Bill continues, "but it's not like some Swiss yodeler. It's really what LeAnn and I call a soul break. It's like something's tuggin' at you."

The year 1993 was a pivotal one for the Rimes family. Wilbur left his job as a salesman to manage his daughter's career. He met Dallas attorney Lyle Walker, who was part owner of a New Mexico studio where Buddy Holly and Roy Orbison had recorded some of their hit records. Lyle financed LeAnn's first album and signed on as her comanager.

It should have been an exciting time for LeAnn, but she was having serious problems in school. While plans for her first album were being finalized, she asked her parents if she could leave school after she finished the sixth grade and have a private tutor.

She was now entering junior high, and school was becoming an unhappy experience for her. Because she was a local star and had been on TV, she says, some kids harassed her, and she was "threatened a lot. I had a lot of friends, but there were these four girls who were scaring me sometimes. I had a rough time. Kids who didn't understand thought I was different from everybody else, which I'm not.

"That was probably the toughest," she continues. "I cried a few times because I didn't understand why they thought I was different. Country artists are just normal people with a certain talent. I never got mad. I kind of understood what they thought, and I was different in ways they didn't understand. But I didn't change, because I enjoyed what I was doing."

A home tutor began helping LeAnn with her

schoolwork every day. The arrangement worked out well. LeAnn continued to maintain a straight-A average. Her favorites were math and English, to which she gave unremitting attention. Her test scores were so high that she was able to skip two grades.

A typical day for LeAnn consisted of three hours of work with her tutor. She spent an additional hour on homework, and the rest of her time was spent working with her father on her music. LeAnn was inching closer and closer to the stardom she so desperately wanted.

Although she did not know it at the time, the key to LeAnn's future career would be the independent album her father was producing. The primary reason for recording the album was to sell it at local concerts. Both Wilbur and LeAnn had no idea that it would jump-start her career, giving it a forward momentum beyond their wildest dreams.

The Rimeses traveled across the state line to Clovis, New Mexico, to begin working on LeAnn's album.

When she walked into the recording studio for the first time, LeAnn was overwhelmed. Above her hung a microphone, and in front of her was a music stand holding the lyrics of her songs. She stood facing her father, who was across from her behind the thick glass of the control booth. Next to Wilbur was a crew of technicians.

Wilbur used a microphone to talk to LeAnn. Because this was an album her father was producing, LeAnn hoped to do a good job. Standing beneath the hanging microphone, she fixed the lyric sheets on the music stand and adjusted her headphones. "We're ready to start recording, LeAnn," her father said. "You're going to do just fine."

LeAnn nodded and cleared her throat. A red light went on. The tape began to run, the music in her headphones started, and LeAnn opened her mouth to sing "Blue." Once the first few notes were out, she began to relax. As she sang, the lingering flutters of anxiety quickly gave way to something more powerful: excitement.

That day, LeAnn recorded the song that would change her life.

The day her first CD was completed was a day of celebration. The album was called *All That*, and the cover showed a cute photo of LeAnn dressed in white fringe and gold sequins. It was released in 1994 on the independent label Nor Va Jak.

At first LeAnn's CD was sold only at her shows. Then Lyle Walker got the Blockbuster Music chain interested in carrying it. In less than one year, more than fifteen thousand copies of *All That* were sold.

Having her CD in Blockbuster without being on a major label gave LeAnn wide exposure. But that was only the beginning. Something even more surprising happened as a result of *All That*.

LeAnn's independent album was selling so well that Nashville came calling. Dubbed Music City, U.S.A., by radio deejay David Cobb in 1950, Nashville is the only place that can give country singers a career that will catapult them to superstardom.

LeAnn Rimes knew this was the step she had to take if she wanted a successful career in country music. She had to get to Nashville and make them believe she could be the next Reba, Dolly, or Tammy.

LeAnn vowed to make this new phase of her life a spectacular one. If she could have known just how spectacularly she would succeed, even she would have been amazed.

5

Out of the Blue

One of the first executives interested in signing LeAnn Rimes to a record deal was Jimmy Bowen, then head of Capitol records in Nashville. Bowen, who had begun his career as a rockabilly and country singer in the late 1950s, had something in common with LeAnn. He did most of his recording at Norman Petty's studio in Clovis, New Mexico, the same place LeAnn had recorded *All That*.

Bowen invited LeAnn to his home in Nashville so that he could listen to her sing and talk about her future career. The trip, however, turned out to be a disappointment for LeAnn. Even though she was happy to meet Jimmy Bowen, she left the meeting with very little encouragement.

"He told me to come back when I was eighteen because he didn't want to take on a child," she says. "He thought I wasn't really old enough to handle. He was right to tell me to wait, but I couldn't. I really wanted it."

LeAnn was ready to embark on a recording career. Unfortunately, that did not happen overnight. During the next two years, she was courted by numerous Nashville record executives and managers. They offered her contracts and promised her stardom. But her father didn't want to rush into anything. Wilbur would only agree to a deal he felt comfortable with.

When LeAnn got to Nashville, the country music business was undergoing many changes. The youth movement of the early 1990s that had turned unknowns like Garth Brooks and Alan Jackson into superstars was reaching its peak. Nashville record executives put out the word that they wanted to sign younger artists. They were hoping to get teenagers interested in buying country music albums by signing hot, young, good-looking singers.

LeAnn was at the right place at the right time in country music history. Contemporary country had become the growth area of the music business. With the introduction of a new generation of artists, the popularity of contemporary country grew while other genres slumped.

Country music today has moved much closer

to pop but still has country flavor. The stereotypical sound associated with old-time country is gone. There are fewer whining steel guitars, high-pitched nasal vocals, twanging banjos, and twin fiddles. Performers have deliberately smoothed their rough singing edges and toned down their distinctive instrumentation.

By 1993 country artists were in vogue with pop fans. Country music was the most listened-to format on the radio, with stations springing up all over the United States and sales of country albums at an all-time high.

Where fifty thousand sales of an album had once constituted a major hit, artists were now selling millions of audio and video products. According to the Recording Industry Association of America, sales in country music grew from $425 million in 1988 to more than $2 billion in 1995.

Several breakout stars contributed to country's rise in popularity. Billy Ray Cyrus's history-making first album, *Some Gave All*, became the best-selling debut disc of all time, eventually selling twelve million copies worldwide. Shania Twain's sophomore release, *The Woman in Me*, spent an unprecedented twenty-nine weeks at number one and has sold more than ten million copies.

And then there is Garth Brooks, the biggest country superstar of them all. He broke records previously set by pop icons Billy Joel, Elton John, and the Eagles. In just seven years, Brooks has sold more records than any other artist except the Beatles. At more than sixty million units sold, he is the best-selling solo artist of all time, and clearly the star who helped transform country music into the entertainment industry's hottest commodity.

The next step for country seemed obvious: to break into the teen market. In 1994 twenty-year-old Bryan White soared onto the charts with his debut release and became a favorite with teenage girls. As country's first teen idol, Bryan was enjoying a red-hot career. He would ultimately open the door for other young artists.

In 1994 labels started scouting for new talent. They were eager to sign artists in their early twenties—or even younger if possible. At twelve years old, LeAnn Rimes was perfect. Nashville leaders and managers were clamoring to sign her. She stood on the threshold of stardom. But she had to be patient.

After Jimmy Bowen turned LeAnn down, Decca expressed interest in her. Decca had been a leading label in country music all through the 1950s and 1960s. Legendary artists like Patsy Cline, Loretta Lynn, and Conway Twitty all recorded for Decca. But the label's name was retired in 1973 when MCA bought it out. In 1994 MCA decided to resurrect the Decca name and announced it was in the market for new artists.

Executives from the Decca label wanted to add LeAnn to their roster. They flew to Dallas to meet with her and her parents. After LeAnn had performed for them in a Dallas theater, they told Wilbur they wanted to sign her.

But when Decca presented its deal, Wilbur wasn't satisfied with what the label was promising. He decided to hold out until the right deal came along. He knew he had plenty of time. LeAnn was only twelve years old, and he didn't want her to get caught up in anything he didn't approve of.

While talks with Decca went back and forth, manager Narvel Blackstock contacted Wilbur Rimes. Narvel, who is Reba McEntire's husband and head of Reba's Starstruck Management Company, was eager to sign a hot new talent like LeAnn. Up to that point, Narvel was managing the gospel quartet 4 Runner, rising country star Linda Davis, and up-and-coming singer Rhett Aikens, and was having only minor success.

Narvel wanted LeAnn to join the growing Starstruck family, but Wilbur decided not to sign with Narvel. He didn't want someone else managing his daughter's career. Instead, Wilbur set up his own management company with Lyle Walker back home in Dallas. Together they would continue to guide LeAnn in the right musical direction.

In the spring of 1995 Wilbur was contacted by the man who would eventually launch LeAnn's career. Mike Curb, the owner and president of Curb Records, Nashville's largest and most influential independent label, was on the lookout for a new singer. Mike Curb recalls that he knew LeAnn was star material the second he heard her sing.

"Someone sent me her CD," he says. "I was leaving town with my family to drive up to the Smoky Mountains. I have two daughters about LeAnn's age. When I put her CD on, everyone just turned their heads and said, 'Who is that?'

"We played it all the way up and all the way back, over and over. On the way home, I stopped at a pay phone and called her management and said, 'We are interested in this artist very much.' "

Mike Curb, a major figure in the music business, worked with the top teen stars of the late 1960s and 1970s in both pop and country. He was the driving force behind the careers of major idols of the day such as Shaun Cassidy, Debby Boone, Hank Williams, Jr., the Osmond Brothers, and Marie Osmond. Once called the "boy wonder" of the music business, Curb made a career out of finding young singers and single-handedly launching them into superstardom.

When he heard LeAnn's CD, he knew he had stumbled across someone he could mold into the next big thing in country music. He was ready to sign LeAnn to his label, and nothing was going to stand in his way. He made Wilbur an offer he couldn't refuse.

For one thing, Mike promised Wilbur that

LeAnn's management could remain in the family. Mike was ready to give LeAnn his undivided attention. He was also ready to sign LeAnn to a multialbum deal.

Some labels were giving new artists one-time album deals. If their debut album did not do well, they were being released from their contracts before getting the chance to prove their talents on a second album. Unlike the bigger labels in town, Curb Records gave its artists a chance to grow as performers even if their first album wasn't the hit the label had anticipated.

LeAnn and her dad were convinced this was the right label for her. LeAnn says, "We would have a little more control of my career if we did it this way."

In May 1995, after two years of negotiations, LeAnn signed her first major-label contract with Curb Records. She was given one year to work on her album. Mike Curb made it clear that he was in no hurry to push her out into the public eye just yet.

LeAnn liked the arrangement. She had all the time in the world to work on her music and get it right before anyone had heard it. Only two songs were taken off her independent album. She rerecorded "Blue," her father says, "to fit her thirteen-year-old voice." And the ballad "I'll Get Even with You" from *All That* was updated and added to her Curb Records project.

The period between May 1995 and April 1996 was a fun and exhilarating time for LeAnn. She was so immersed in her music that she even started to dabble in songwriting. The process fascinated her. She wrote a few songs with the help of composers Ron Grimes and Jon Rutherford. One of them, "Talk to Me," was recorded for her debut album. She was so excited that she started composing other songs; she hopes to include them on future albums.

LeAnn felt strongly about the type of material she wanted to record. It was decided that her first album would be a combination of the old and new Nashville sounds. It was an ingenious idea, one that would differentiate LeAnn's album from others.

Some songs chosen were traditional in style, like "Blue," "Honestly," and "Fade to Blue." There were also a few up-tempo songs, like the bright and bouncy "One Way Ticket (Because I Can)" and the snappy "Good Lookin' Man."

LeAnn chose to record "Hurt Me" and "My Baby," both written by singer and songwriter Deborah Allen. "I'm a big fan of Deborah Allen," says LeAnn. "I have all her albums. I'm glad I recorded two of her songs for my album. 'Hurt Me' is one of my favorite songs. I think she's one of the best songwriters in Nashville."

Mike Curb came up with the idea of having LeAnn perform the classic song "Cattle Call," which had been a number one hit in 1955 for Eddy Arnold. Mike was hoping the legendary artist would agree to come out of retirement and rerecord his song as a duet with LeAnn.

One afternoon after Mike had had lunch with Eddy Arnold, Mike popped LeAnn's tape into his cassette player. "When I heard it, I said, 'Gosh, that little gal can really sing,' " remembers Eddy, who next asked her name.

Mike told him LeAnn's name and explained she had just turned thirteen years old. He then told Eddy Arnold that she would be recording a remake of "Cattle Call" for her album. He asked if Eddy would consider coming into the studio and cutting it as a duet with LeAnn.

It didn't take the seventy-eight-year-old country star long to give Mike an answer. He said he'd love to. It would be only the second duet Eddy Arnold had recorded in his fifty-year career. His first was "Mutual Admiration Society," a 1956 duet with pop singer Jaye P. Morgan.

To say LeAnn was excited about singing with Eddy Arnold is an understatement. "I was thrilled!" she says. "He was wonderful. He kind of adopted me, first as his granddaughter, then as his daughter. He's a very, very nice guy."

LeAnn felt fortunate to be combining her talents with those of the great country artist. In the liner notes of her album, LeAnn wrote a special thank-you: "What an honor to sing with such a great man and a living legend."

Eddy was equally happy to sing with LeAnn, who, he says, has "one of the best voices I ever heard."

LeAnn recorded the tracks for her album in four different studios: Norman Petty's studio in Clovis, New Mexico; Rosewood Studio in Tyler, Texas; Mid-Town Tone & Volume and Omni Sound in Nashville.

While LeAnn was still putting the final touches on her album, Curb Records began early promotion to make people aware of her. Press releases alerted the media to LeAnn's first solo effort.

In late April 1996, Curb Records released a four-song sampler to radio stations. The sampler included "Blue," "The Light in Your Eyes," "Hurt Me," and "My Baby." Originally Curb Records had planned to release "The Light in Your Eyes" as the first single, but the company switched to "Blue" after radio stations had started playing it.

Part of Curb Records' shrewd marketing campaign was to include the story of "Blue" with the sampler. Dene Hallam, program director of Houston's KKBQ, says the station's disc jockeys told the story to listeners every time they played "Blue," which was as often as eight times a day. "It was evident from the second day that it was a phenomenon," says Dene Hallam.

Curb set up a showcase for LeAnn at the Country Radio Seminar in Tampa to introduce her to disc jockeys. Kevin O'Neal of Philadelphia's WXTU remembers that LeAnn performed in front of "a pretty tough room of critics. They had all these risers set up, and I thought, 'They're going to put a thirteen-year-old on there singing to tracks. I don't even want to see the massacre.' " But when LeAnn hit the stage, composed, mature, and oozing with talent and confidence, O'Neal says, "In thirty seconds, we were all spellbound."

Next LeAnn traveled to the Gavin Country Radio Seminar in Los Angeles and the Country Radio Seminar in Dallas. She made a strong impression everywhere she appeared.

Mike Curb was thoroughly pleased with LeAnn. She was pretty and friendly and had the right attitude. The Curb Records publicity department knew it was going to be easy to publicize her.

The first radio stations that decided to give LeAnn's song a spin on the air weren't prepared for the response they received from listeners. "We put it on the air one time and instantly got calls from record stores from people walking in specifically wanting to buy *that* song," says WXTU's Kevin O'Neal. "Originally we were concerned about playing a record that sounds too much like yesterday, but with LeAnn's youth and freshness this record comes home. I can't think of anybody else who could have sung this song and made it work."

When Mac Daniels, program director of WMZQ in Washington, D.C., gave "Blue" a try, he didn't expect listeners to jam the phone lines. "I gave it to our nighttime guy, Scott Carpenter, and said, 'Take this, have some fun with it,' " says Daniels. "He played it that night and the response was so overwhelming, he had to play it three times. It was kids calling, kids' grandparents calling. The next morning, the morning deejay, Gary Murphy, comes to me and says, 'What's this "Blue" song? We're getting a ton of calls. We need to play it.' "

When Daniels decided to pull the song from the playlist that afternoon, more calls lit up the station's switchboard.

Radio programmers agreed they hadn't seen a song become so popular with listeners since Billy Ray Cyrus's "Achy Breaky Heart" and Tim McGraw's "Indian Outlaw." In May 1996 "Blue" broke into the airplay-based *Billboard* country chart at number forty-nine. Five weeks later it was number twelve. It spent two weeks at number ten.

When Charlie Dick, Patsy Cline's widower, heard "Blue" for the first time on his car radio, he had to pull over to the side of the road. "She's got a little bit of a lot of people in her voice," says Charlie of LeAnn. "I hear Patsy. I hear Brenda

Lee. I'm sorry Patsy didn't get to record that song."

Curb Records was thrilled by the news that "Blue" was a hit across the country. According to Karen McGuire, the northeast regional manager for Curb Records and wife of WMZQ's Mac Daniels, LeAnn's song was the second most added record to country station playlists coast to coast.

About "Blue," Steve Lee, promotion director of Curb's southwest region, said, "We're talking about a first week that new artists dream of but only superstars have."

When the single was finally released to retail stores the first week of June, it sold more than a hundred thousand copies and was the number-one-selling single for twenty consecutive weeks. Deana Carter's "Strawberry Wine" eventually knocked it out of the top spot.

When *Entertainment Weekly* reviewed the single "Blue," it said about LeAnn, "This kid—she's only thirteen—has got a voice that'll just knock you out. She sounds just like Patsy Cline. She's gonna go right to the top."

LeAnn was thrilled that "Blue" was a hit. Not long after her single had been released, she expressed her feelings about the song's popularity in an interview. "I think a lot of country music fans who are twenty years old and younger, sort of my age, don't know what the older, traditional country sounds like," LeAnn said. "It's wonderful they're hearing 'Blue' and they're liking it, because it definitely reflects the traditional country sound and where country started. It makes me feel great that all age groups are loving this record."

She went on to say that initially she had been skeptical when "Blue" was released as her debut song. " 'Blue' was very traditional, and I knew radio was going to be hesitant to play it," she said. "It's true country music and totally different from contemporary country, which has the pop feel." Later, she said, "I don't think I would be having this kind of success without 'Blue.' It definitely stood out from everything that was being played on the radio."

By the middle of May, as LeAnn was concentrating on finishing her album, Curb Records was putting a lot of thought into the packaging of her debut release. LeAnn was scheduled to pose for the first set of publicity photos as well as the photos for the album cover.

Up to this point, all phases of putting her album together had gone smoothly. The only difficulty LeAnn encountered was when it came time to choose the cover photo. LeAnn originally wanted the photo to reflect her youth and personality, while the record company wanted a more mature look. Although Curb Records planned to promote LeAnn as a teenage singing star, the company didn't want to alienate older record buyers.

Curb's solution was to have LeAnn appear slightly older on the cover so that it could sell more records. The photograph selected shows a serious LeAnn wearing a long dress with a lace top. It's a very flattering shot taken by Nashville photographer Peter Nash. The people at Curb Records believed the alluring photo of LeAnn would attract *all* record buyers. They would know soon enough whether this was true.

By the time Fan Fair rolled around, the second week of June, it was clear that LeAnn was already hot. She had made a big, splashy entrance onto the music scene. On the strength of her song "Blue," she had already won fans, and they couldn't wait until her album was released. Because of the overwhelming response, the date of LeAnn's debut album was pushed up from September to July.

Curb Records cranked up the publicity machine to full speed in anticipation of LeAnn's first release. She was told to get ready for a whirlwind of interviews and appearances.

There was a large record-buying world out there, and Curb Records wanted to be sure that it knew all about LeAnn Rimes.

6

One-Way Ticket to the Top

On July 9, 1996, only two months after the release of the song "Blue," LeAnn's album, also titled *Blue*, went on sale. The album was an instant success. It blew right past established country superstars George Strait and Garth Brooks and debuted in the number one spot on the *Billboard* country chart. LeAnn landed in the history books as the youngest country singer ever to have a debut album hit the top spot in the first week of release.

It was big news in Nashville. Music Row was buzzing about the fact that LeAnn's album knocked out Shania Twain's previously unbeatable *The Woman in Me*, which had been number one for a total of twenty-nine weeks. No one else had been able to pull that off, never mind a thirteen-year-old newcomer!

With all of this happening, LeAnn was on a concert tour. "I was out on the road between performances when *Blue* was released," she says. "People at the label kept telling me my album could debut at number one, but I was real skeptical. Then it did—and I couldn't believe it! It's humbling that my album may make country music history. It's humbling and it's cool."

Even more surprising to LeAnn was that her album simultaneously debuted at number four on *Billboard*'s pop chart. Prince's new album, *Chaos and Disorder*, was released the same week as *Blue*. But his album sold a disappointing 38,000 copies and went as high as number twenty-six. SoundScan reported that *Blue* sold an astronomical 124,000 copies in its first week of release.

According to LeAnn, getting onto the country charts was expected, but debuting on the pop charts "was unbelievable. The news made me excited and happy!" Her album would eventually go up as high as number three on the pop charts, one notch above powerhouse rockers like Metallica, and would stay in the Top 20 for the next six months.

Blue was a towering achievement for LeAnn. She was thrilled with it, and so were the people who rushed out to buy it. Everyone seemed to find something to love about LeAnn's debut disc.

Blue is brilliant, filled with compelling and powerful songs. Although most country albums include the standard ten songs, LeAnn broke tradition by recording eleven tracks. "We couldn't decide which song to leave out," she says. "So we put all eleven on the album."

The album begins with her signature song, "Blue." That's followed up with Deborah Allen's "Hurt Me," a beautiful torch song that LeAnn sings with passion.

The album is peppered with powerful ballads and catchy pop-oriented country tunes. "One Way Ticket (Because I Can)," the third cut on the album and LeAnn's big number one single, is one of the album's best songs. Written by Judy Rodman and Keith Hinton, it is upbeat and hummable, and it shows off LeAnn's youth and vibrance. Listening to this song, it's apparent that LeAnn had a lot of fun singing it.

Most of the songs on the album are about love. The sultry "My Baby" has a terrific country rock sound. Written by Deborah Allen, it begins with the crisp strum of a guitar.

On the melodic "Honestly," written by Christi Dannemiller and Joe Johnston, LeAnn sings of a relationship rumored to be over.

On Dan Tyler's lively song "The Light in Your Eyes," she takes each note and embraces it.

"Talk to Me," the song she wrote with Ron Grimes and Jon Rutherford, contains a potent blend of country and a pop sound. LeAnn's vocal performance is extremely expressive. As one of the songwriters of this tune, LeAnn also shows another side of her endless talent.

"I'll Get Even with You" returns the album to a softer mood and slower tempo. This song holds a special place in LeAnn's heart. "I love it," she proclaims. "I had the song on my independent album and was glad everyone agreed to put it on *Blue.*" Written by Coweta House, "I'll Get Even with You" is a delicious song that emphasizes LeAnn's distinctive sound.

The classic "Cattle Call," her duet with Eddy Arnold, confirms that LeAnn's voice is one of the best in Nashville. After she lets loose on the rollicking "Good Lookin' Man," her album ends with the haunting "Fade to Blue." With piano, guitar, and drums playing behind her, she sings the heart-wrenching story of a couple breaking up. In this simmering song of lost love, LeAnn turns in a superb performance.

Once *Blue* had been released, the reviews started pouring in, but LeAnn didn't want to read any of them. She was so happy with her album that she didn't want anything to put a damper on it. Her father read all the early reviews and put her mind at ease. The album was unanimously praised. Some called LeAnn the year's brightest new artist.

Newsday said about *Blue*, "Nothing kidlike

about it, Rimes' is a voice that is mature and highly nuanced. LeAnn Rimes rises to greatness. *Blue* is a classic."

Critics were calling LeAnn's first effort one of the best new albums to come out of Nashville in years. *USA Today* said, "LeAnn Rimes can emote with the best of them, and she has a retro style. Her carefully balanced duet with seventy-eight-year-old Eddy Arnold on 'Cattle Call' gives notice that this youngster has good musical sense and is here to stay."

The headline in *The Dallas Morning News* was " 'Blue' isn't a bunch of nursery Rimes. Teenage country crooner sounds like an old hand."

Everyone was in agreement: LeAnn Rimes had a hit album and was being hailed as a star. But she was bowled over by a rush of different emotions at the news that her album had debuted at the top. While she was obviously ecstatic about the success of her debut release, she felt challenged and pressured. Because she was only thirteen, she was afraid the industry was going to regard her as a one-hit wonder or a novelty act.

There was so much riding on her album that it made LeAnn feel overly self-critical. She found herself thinking that the song "Blue" might have been a fluke, that she might not achieve success with the rest of the album's singles.

For a time, LeAnn's suspicions seemed to be on target. In July radio stations suddenly pulled

"Blue" from their playlists with no explanation. Luckily the radio snub didn't hurt the sales of the single. Still, no one knows for sure what had happened. In late May stations across the country were spinning "Blue" as often as 1,126 times a day. By July, it was down to only a few times a day in certain markets.

Industry insiders blamed it on the fact that some programmers were not comfortable playing a traditional-sounding record. Program director Renee Revett of KXKC in Lafayette, Louisiana, says, "It didn't sound like the kind of country music we were playing in 1996." Others said "Blue" had had its day. But Dennis Hannon of Curb Records says, "To this day, whenever the song is played, the voice, the sound just leaps out of the radio at you."

Curb Records decided to rush out the album's second song, "Hurt Me," as LeAnn's next single. But the song had received only mediocre airplay and had practically no chart action. What may have hurt the song is that it was a remake. Deborah Allen, who wrote the song, had recorded it on her album *All That I Am* in 1994. Also, as another ballad, it is similar to "Blue." Reports came in that radio was giving "Hurt Me" the cold shoulder, but LeAnn was rising above it—although she was clearly disappointed.

By summer's end, the third single from *Blue* was rushed to radio stations and retail stores.

LeAnn with Bill Mack, the Texas disc jockey who wrote her signature song, "Blue." Bill Mack says, "She did the song exactly the way I wanted it done." It was LeAnn's idea to add the yodel to the song. (Copyright © 1997 by Zuma)

"My biggest goal is to keep recording the best music I can, go out and do the best concerts, and take it day by day," says LeAnn, thinking about her future. (Copyright © 1997 by Zuma)

"Here's the bright future of country music, Miss LeAnn Rimes," said Vince Gill as he introduced LeAnn on the 1996 CMA Awards. LeAnn opened the show and got it off to a great start. (Copyright © 1996 by Alan L. Mayor)

LeAnn and her dad, Wilbur, are very close. He is LeAnn's manager and has been beside her every step of the way. "I'm so lucky because my parents helped me reach my dreams," says LeAnn. (Copyright © 1996 by Scott Downie/Celebrity Photo)

"Having a hit record is exciting," says LeAnn. "But the success of 'Blue' didn't happen overnight. Even though things have fallen into place fast, I've been singing since I was five and I've worked hard!" (Copyright © 1996 by Connie Ives/Hot Shot Photos)

Whether she's wearing jeans, designer dresses, or this sparkling blue outfit, vivacious LeAnn looks terrific in everything. (Copyright © 1996 by Alan L. Mayor)

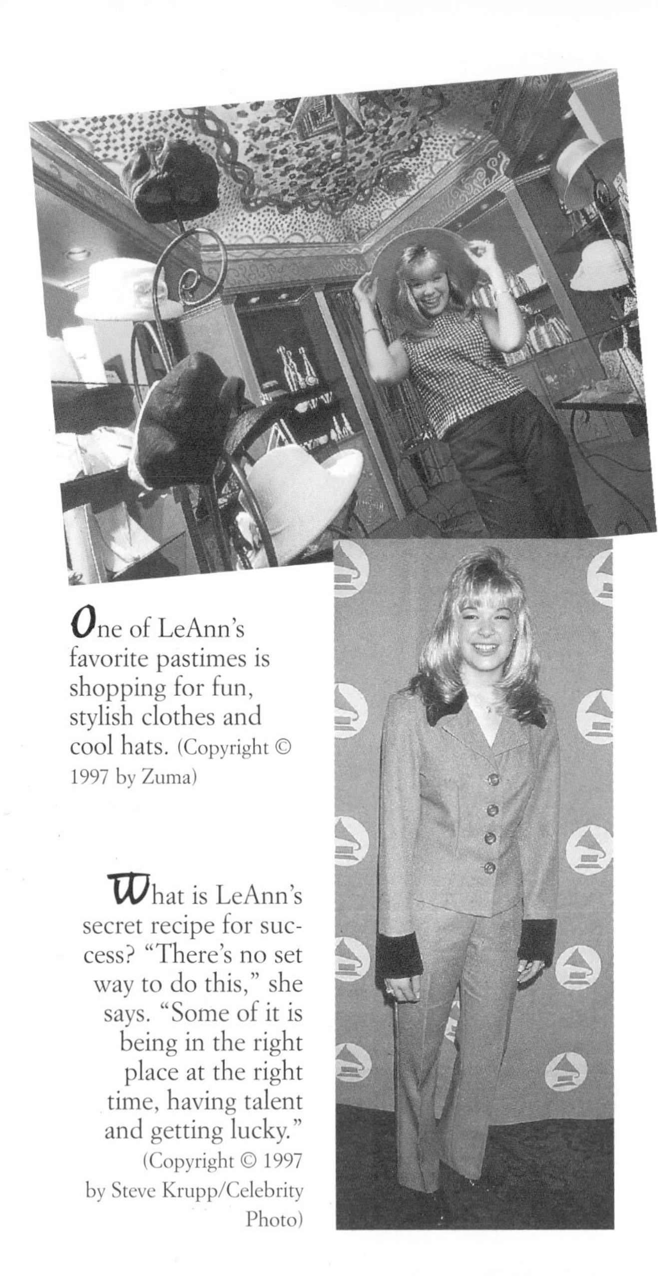

One of LeAnn's favorite pastimes is shopping for fun, stylish clothes and cool hats. (Copyright © 1997 by Zuma)

What is LeAnn's secret recipe for success? "There's no set way to do this," she says. "Some of it is being in the right place at the right time, having talent and getting lucky." (Copyright © 1997 by Steve Krupp/Celebrity Photo)

At her first Fan Fair, LeAnn stepped onstage and drove the crowd wild. The pretty country singer has taken the music world by storm! (Copyright © 1996 by Alan L. Mayor)

Country music's top teen dream girl takes a sip of a strawberry ice cream soda, her favorite dessert. (Copyright © 1997 by Zuma)

LeAnn was the holiday spokesperson for Target stores across the nation. She was happy to ride on the Target float in the 1996 Hollywood Christmas Parade. (Copyright © 1996 by Connie Ives/Hot Shot Photos)

When LeAnn steps out of the glare of the spotlight, she craves a quiet, casual lifestyle free from worries. This typical teenager enjoys riding cutting horses, tennis, swimming, and going to see her favorite stars in concert. (Copyright © 1997 by Zuma)

LeAnn with talk show hosts Lorianne Crook and Charlie Chase at the opening of the Country Star American Grill Restaurant in Las Vegas. (Copyright © 1996 by Bob Ives/Hot Shot Photos)

Photographers snap LeAnn wherever she goes—and she's always ready to flash her winning smile. (Copyright © 1996 by Bob Ives/Hot Shot Photos)

*A*t the 1996 CMA Awards, LeAnn and Marty Stuart inducted Patsy Montana into the Country Music Hall of Fame. (Copyright © 1996 by Alan L. Mayor)

"*I* love going out onstage and seeing the fans," says LeAnn. "It's really neat to see them singing along with my songs." (Copyright © 1996 by Alan L. Mayor)

Curb Records released the album's third cut, "One Way Ticket (Because I Can)," as LeAnn's third single.

"Hurt Me" may have broken LeAnn's winning streak, but "One Way Ticket" sent her soaring to the top. The sizzling single became LeAnn's first number one smash hit on all the *Billboard* charts. LeAnn struck gold with this song. It placed her name in the country music history books as the youngest performer to have a number one song *and* album on the charts at the same time.

As her third single vaulted to the top of the charts, it was apparent that LeAnn's winning voice and attitude were the two things making her a star. She was welcomed with open arms by fans, the media, and top entertainment figures. Throughout the summer of 1996, LeAnn was the hottest new music star in the country. She had emerged as a major celebrity.

As her album continued to break records, LeAnn began appearing on TV talk shows and gave countless interviews to radio stations, newspapers, and magazines. She didn't have a minute to call her own.

"Everyone is starting to know who I am," she announced in an interview. People were beginning to pay a lot of attention to LeAnn. Her name and face began popping up everywhere. But for all the positive things happening, LeAnn wasn't exempt from a little controversy.

Interviewers questioned her about her age. There were reports that she was actually a decade older. One tabloid story reported that LeAnn wasn't a teenager at all, but was actually a thirty-one-year-old Asian woman. Now LeAnn laughs about the stories that were circulating, but at the time it was a problem.

"People started asking me if they could see my driver's license," says LeAnn. "And I would tell them, 'I don't *have* one. I couldn't *get* one. Then they asked, 'Can we see your birth certificate?' And I said, 'I don't have it on me.' "

LeAnn and her parents were faced with the dilemma of having to convince the public that she was *really* only thirteen years old. Belinda decided to enlarge LeAnn's birth certificate and show it on national television. The Rimeses chose the show *Entertainment Tonight* to unveil the proof of LeAnn's age.

Next came a new controversy. LeAnn was coming under fire for recording love songs that many people believed spoke of life experiences way beyond hers. LeAnn made it clear that she is the interpreter of the songs she sings. "I don't think I have to experience anything to sing these songs," she said in one interview. "It's like an actor playing out a part they haven't lived. If I fall in love with the music and the overall song, I just think, 'I want to sing that.' I might not have lived it, but I know what it's about, so I can basically feel the song. I've seen people get hurt before. My close friends have gotten hurt, and I know what they're going through."

It was LeAnn who chose many of the songs on her album. She deliberately set out to record songs people could relate to. "What I wanted to do with my album was keep it traditional and contemporary country so it would be a wide spectrum for everyone."

Regardless of her young age, she chose not to sing "little kid songs about getting out of high school." As she puts it, "I'm trying to appeal to everyone from age four to eighty."

LeAnn has certainly accomplished everything she set out to do. The success of *Blue* changed her life forever. At the ripe old age of thirteen, she was already established as a major recording artist, with her album continuing to sell an amazing 125,000 copies every week. That may never be equaled by another country artist—especially one so young.

On August 28, 1996, the day LeAnn turned fourteen, she received the best birthday present of her life. Her album had sold an incredible 815,000 copies and was certified gold.

It was only the beginning. *Blue* would go on to become the biggest seller of the year, and LeAnn Rimes was being called the hottest singer in American music.

7

A Family Affair

LeAnn's busiest year—packed with talk show appearances, concert dates, and photo sessions—was 1996. Keeping her on schedule through the year and into 1997 were the two most important people in her life: her parents, Wilbur and Belinda.

LeAnn describes her parents "as the biggest influence in my life," adding that if it weren't for them, she wouldn't be where she is today. Because the Rimeses put a family effort into LeAnn's career from the start, it has made her newfound popularity easier for her to handle.

Johnnie High had come to know the Rimes family very well in the days when LeAnn sang in his Country Music Revue. He had witnessed LeAnn's ambitions and her parents' support. "Her parents saw this coming a long time ago," he says of LeAnn's success. "They're prepared."

Despite her sudden stardom, LeAnn has kept a level head. "I haven't had time to think about it," she says. "I know I'm only fourteen, but I've been working very hard for a long time and I know what I went through to get here. I think that's what keeps me grounded.

"They tell me I sell a hundred and twenty-five thousand albums in a week," she continues, "and I say, 'That's really neat,' and go on about my business. It's what I do. No matter what you do, no matter how good you are, you can always improve."

People might think LeAnn must be spoiled by all the attention she receives, but it's clear that she remains very modest about her career. Her seemingly overpowering success has not affected her at all.

Because LeAnn can communicate with her parents on any topic, the three Rimeses enjoy a strong family relationship. "I'm very lucky," says LeAnn. "Whenever I have a problem, I can talk to my parents about anything."

In 1994 the lives of LeAnn and her parents were turned upside down. While they were in the midst of traveling back and forth to and from Nashville, trying to work out the legalities of getting LeAnn a record deal, they learned that Belinda's mother, Annie Jewell Butler, had died.

LeAnn took the news especially hard because she was very close to her grandmother. When she was little, LeAnn used to go over to her grandmother's house, put on her old records, and sing along. Annie always knew LeAnn would go far and always gave her strong encouragement.

Heartbroken, LeAnn promised herself that she would give her grandmother a special dedication in her first album.

Inside *Blue* LeAnn wrote, "I dedicate this album to my Grandfather, Thad Butler, along with a very special dedication to my Grandmother, Annie Jewell Butler, who passed away in 1994. I love you, Maw Maw!"

It was a very difficult time for LeAnn and her parents. But they managed to get through it. In some ways, it made LeAnn more determined than ever to succeed.

According to Belinda, "LeAnn is, and always has been, focused. She would go over you, through you, around you to do what she is doing right now."

Because LeAnn achieved her goal at such a young age, her parents have had to work hard to adjust to her success. "Having a child in show business involves all of us," says Belinda in a soft voice. "My job right now is to keep her head on straight, keep her honorable. She's a God-given child with a God-given talent."

Belinda remarks that all the attention LeAnn receives is very flattering but hasn't prevented her from worrying about her daughter. "I worry all the time," she admits. "Children in this business grow up faster because they are in situations where they're expected to work as an adult. They're in an adult environment, yet they're still really children, so it can be difficult."

To make LeAnn's life and career easier, both her parents keep a watchful eye on her. After the runaway success of her album, the phone started ringing off the hook with requests for interviews. Because of the tremendous demands on his daughter's time, Wilbur decided he had to reject some of the requests. It was just impossible for LeAnn to fit everything into her busy schedule.

As the manager of LeAnn's career, Wilbur tries to make the best business decisions for her. As her father, he carefully monitors the amount of work she does. LeAnn's health and well-being are all that matters to him.

"She's in such demand, I had to turn some interviews and appearances down," he says. "She's too young to push that way." LeAnn knows how much her father cares, and she wouldn't do anything unless he agreed to it. The morning deejays Gary Murphy and Jessica Cash from the Washington, D.C., radio station

WMZQ remember what happened the day they invited LeAnn to appear on a country music event the station was hosting. All Wilbur knew was that Gary and Jessica were going to interview LeAnn—and that was all LeAnn was prepared for.

When they phoned her for a chat on the air, she handled the conversation like a seasoned pro. But when the deejays invited LeAnn to appear on the station's annual Bull Run Country Jamboree, she handed the phone to her father. Wilbur talked to the surprised deejays for a few seconds and agreed to let LeAnn perform at the event.

The Bull Run Country Jamboree is famous for having helped to launch the career of Garth Brooks. Garth made one of his first appearances at the event in the late 1980s and was a big hit with audiences. Now it seemed as if country music history was repeating itself.

Thousands of LeAnn's fans showed up at the Bull Run Country Jamboree to see her show. Other country stars on the bill were Little Texas, Collin Raye, Aaron Tippin, and Jeff Carson. LeAnn was just as excited as the fans to see the other artists perform.

Another event that LeAnn was glad she attended was the grand opening of the Country Star American Music Grill in Las Vegas. This opening of the second restaurant in the country-theme chain was star-studded. LeAnn met her idol Reba McEntire, as well as Vince Gill, Trisha Yearwood, Tracy Lawrence, and John Berry. Walking down the red carpet, LeAnn waved to the fans and stopped to talk to country hosts Lorianne Crook and Charlie Chase, who are celebrity representatives of the restaurant along with Reba, Vince, and Wynonna.

LeAnn couldn't believe she was actually part of such a night. She was as awestruck as the fans who braved the 100-degree heat to get a glimpse of the stars. The highlight of the evening was a miniconcert led by LeAnn singing "Blue." Bryan White and Neal McCoy teamed up for "Going, Going, Gone." Vince Gill and Lee Roy Parnell did two songs, "You Better Think Twice" and "What the Cowgirls Do." Trish Yearwood sang "Rocky Top" with Lee Roy. The show ended on a rousing note when Tracy Lawrence and Kenny Chesney did their version of "Okie from Muskogee."

While her night at the Country Star restaurant opening rates high on LeAnn's list as one of the most memorable nights of her life, she says her favorite trip was going to New York.

She was scheduled to appear on various morning talk shows. But her appearance on *The Late Show with David Letterman* was the most thrilling.

The thought of performing on Letterman's show in the heart of New York City was so exciting to LeAnn that she couldn't imagine how she'd feel: confident or petrified. When the big moment came, she was a little of both but came out of it shining like a star. LeAnn had a genuine way of connecting with every member of the audience. This appearance was very important to her, and she was glad it went so smoothly.

As LeAnn has rocketed to stardom, Wilbur has had a crash course in the ins and outs of the music business. He and his partner, Lyle Walker, opened an office in Dallas, where they manage LeAnn's career. They call their company LeAnn Rimes Entertainment, Inc.

There's no doubt that Wilbur has had the biggest hand in shaping LeAnn's career. From the moment he first made home recordings of her singing to his production of her albums today, he has been her most tireless and effective advocate. Wilbur and LeAnn share the same visions for her future and always have. Instead of resenting his efforts, LeAnn thanks him wholeheartedly for all the hard work he has put into her career. She knows how much her folks gave up so that she could pursue a career, and she knows how lucky she's been to have her family support her. "She's forever reminding us that we're a special part of her life," explains Belinda.

LeAnn directly attributes her love of recording to her interaction with her father as producer. She says she loves the fact that he produces and helps to create her albums. "I can't imagine working with anyone else except my dad," she says.

The Rimes operation is said to have a down-home feel. Wilbur still writes the band's setlists in a spiral notebook, and Belinda feels compelled to mother LeAnn *and* the members of her band. "My mom helps out with everything," says LeAnn. Belinda helps with the unpacking and makes sure everyone is eating right and getting plenty of rest.

Wilbur's main concern is that everyone gets along. And they do, like one big, happy family. Steel guitarist Junior Knight says about LeAnn, "We're not going to let her date until she's forty." Bass player Curtis Randall laughs, "We're the only band with a curfew."

LeAnn is fortunate to have people around her who care about her. Still too young to make contract decisions without her parents, she says with conviction, "I think I'll always go to them even when I get older. I respect their judgment, and know they'll always guide me in the right direction."

LeAnn gets her sensitivity, responsibility, and sincerity from her mother; her father endowed her with a keen sense for business. "I'm very involved in the business part of my career," she says. "That's one thing I don't stay out of. I want to know everything that's going on."

One thing that is kept in the Rimes family is

LeAnn's fan club, which Belinda runs. When the letters started pouring in from admirers wanting to join LeAnn's club, Belinda found herself working full-time sending out fan club kits.

LeAnn thinks it's "so cool to have fans" and enjoys developing a relationship with the people who buy her records or come to see her in concert. LeAnn's club gives its members an opportunity to have direct contact with her. Belinda makes sure all the fans who join are one hundred percent satisfied.

The annual dues are fifteen dollars; for this, LeAnn's fans receive an autographed eight-by-ten-inch photograph, four newsletters a year, a membership card, and up-to-date concert information. With the newsletters, fans also receive details of new and different products. Devoted club members can order from a vast array of merchandise, including T-shirts, key rings, songbooks, photos, and posters.

Running the club has become a labor of love for Belinda. She enjoys corresponding with her daughter's many fans and reading their letters and cards. In only a few months, fifteen hundred fans joined LeAnn's club. "It's fantastic," says Belinda. "We never expected this many people to join in such a short time."

With her mother running her fan club and her father managing her career, LeAnn is sure to have a long and successful run.

Her parents have always been there for LeAnn—and always will be. Wilbur's longtime motto says a great deal: "The family that plays together stays together." Wherever LeAnn's work takes her, her parents go too. Because of their love and support, LeAnn is happy to say she is part of a wonderful family.

"The most important thing in your life is your family," she says. "I'm so lucky because my parents helped me to reach my dreams. They gave me the drive and state of mind to go the distance. They don't mind traveling with me everywhere. We love being together!"

8

On the Road with LeAnn

LeAnn Rimes is hot on a record, but she's even hotter onstage. Her concerts are simply dynamite. She loves performing live and says the feeling she gets when she's playing for her fans is "beyond comparison. There's nothing that can compare to how I feel after I get off the stage. The concerts are the ultimate for me."

After attending one of LeAnn's electrifying shows, many concertgoers feel exactly the same way. LeAnn is a performer who maintains a one-on-one relationship with her audience. When she's singing, she makes every person believe she is singing directly to him or her.

It's obvious that LeAnn enjoys what she's doing, and her high spirits are infectious. To her, the most important element is her performance, and the audience's applause and cheers only make her want to do more.

"I love going out onstage and seeing the fans," she says. "It's really neat to see them singing along with my songs."

Getting ready for a show is sometimes an all-day affair. The scene backstage before a LeAnn Rimes concert is hectic. Band members are tuning their instruments, and the soundman is making sure all the amplifiers and microphones work properly. When LeAnn performs at night, lighting technicians are checking lights. To get her voice in tip-top shape, LeAnn warms up by yodeling.

A LeAnn Rimes concert is the most amazing show anyone could see. Not only does she perform her own string of knock-'em-dead songs, but she also throws in classic pop and country hits. Onstage, she's completely confident; she begins her show by singing "Blue Moon of Kentucky" a cappella. From the moment she starts to sing, LeAnn draws her audience in. Once the applause starts, it doesn't stop until the show is over.

To keep her shows fresh, LeAnn performs songs from her album and tries out new material. Between songs, she chats with her audience. "One song I try to sing at every show is 'Stand by Me,' she says. "That song is definitely one of my favorite oldies!" She also likes to sing Patsy Cline's songs. "I've done 'Crazy' and 'If You've Got Leaving on Your Mind,' " she says. "But I'll probably keep changing. Patsy recorded a lot of songs, and I'd like to sing them all."

When her show is over, LeAnn leaves the stage, but her cheering fans usually call her back for encores. LeAnn begins and ends her shows by singing without musical accompaniment. She often performs Dolly Parton's "I Will Always Love You" as her encore.

When she performed at the annual Country Jam U.S.A. held in Wisconsin in July 1996, more than thirty thousand country fans cheered when her name was announced. With the blistering sun beating down, LeAnn belted out her songs and drove the crowd wild. She was such a hit that they demanded she return to the stage for *two* encores.

It sounds exhausting, but LeAnn is a trouper. "Every time I walk out onstage, no matter how tired I am, I'm always pumped for it," she says. "The minute I see the audience, the adrenaline starts flowing and it's a lot of fun for me. The concerts are definitely the part of each day that I really enjoy and love to do."

After every show, LeAnn stays for as long as two hours to meet and greet her fans one by one. Members of her fan club and winners of radio station contests wait on a long line to meet their favorite star. LeAnn has a huge teenage following but is admired by people of all ages.

LeAnn would never disappoint anyone who wants to meet her backstage. "My fans are important to me," she asserts. "I have a lot of fun with them. I know it's important to give something back to the fans who support my career."

During the summer of 1996, with LeAnn's album ruling the country charts, she embarked on her first full-time concert tour. Her schedule was filled to the brim with appearances as she crisscrossed the country, traveling from one venue to another. By the end of August, she had played more than a hundred concert dates, with more being added for the fall.

Country tours are different from rock tours in that country performers play more dates. A country tour will play as many county fairs and amusement parks as bigger venues. These shows expose singers to a large group of record buyers who may not have the money or time to go to big stadiums. According to LeAnn, playing the fairs and parks is more fulfilling, especially since her younger fans get a chance to see her show.

Although she's there to work, LeAnn looks forward to playing amusement parks so she can spend the day checking out the rides. A bit of a thrill-seeker, LeAnn is a typical teen who likes to test roller coasters and other scary rides whenever she gets the chance. When she performed at Six Flags Over Texas in Arlington, LeAnn was spotted riding all the park's most spine-tingling rides until the park closed.

LeAnn's first year of concerts took her to many interesting locations. She headlined many of her own shows and also opened for other country stars like Wynonna, Vince Gill, Dwight Yoakam, and Tracy Lawrence. Traveling on the road with some of her idols was certainly a major perk for LeAnn.

"We opened four shows with Wynonna in August, and I got to spend some time with her," says LeAnn, who is a big fan. "She called me her little sister—I'll take that!"

The artists who have met or worked with LeAnn have nothing but praise for her. Vince Gill called her "the real deal. So much of it is smoke and mirrors these days, and she's quite refreshing. It makes you feel secure about the future."

One of the most important stops on LeAnn's tour was her debut performance at the world-famous Grand Ole Opry in Nashville. She was scheduled to appear on Friday, September 13. It was the luckiest day of her life.

"It's a big thrill for me to sing on this stage where so many greats have been," she said in an interview before the show. "Just the tradition of the Grand Old Opry is a big thing. You know you've made it when you get to come on the Grand Ole Opry."

From the minute LeAnn and her parents walked through the backstage entrance, the Opry house was filled with anticipation. Opry stars, staff and crew, backstage guests, and band members waited in the wings to hear country music's youngest star perform.

LeAnn's Opry appearance was spectacular. Introduced by veteran Opry member Jeannie Seely, LeAnn strolled out onto the legendary stage and opened with "Blue." Bob Whittaker, who had invited LeAnn to sing at the Opry at Fan Fair two months earlier, gave her a fifteen-minute spot on the show.

As photographers' flashes lit up the stage, LeAnn, dressed in light green pants with a short matching jacket, sang her heart out. Between songs, she smiled dazzlingly and told the audience, "It's been a lifelong dream since I was really little to sing on the Opry."

She demonstrated her yodeling abilities on "I Want to Be a Cowboy's Sweetheart." Then, as a tribute to Bill Monroe, she performed an up-tempo, rocking version of Monroe's classic "Blue Moon of Kentucky."

But that wasn't the end of her extraordinary night. The highlight came when Mike Curb walked onstage. Carrying two plaques, one in each hand, he surprised LeAnn by presenting her with a gold *and* a platinum record at the same time for her number one album. LeAnn could barely contain her emotions. She spotted her parents off to the side of the stage watching her accept her plaques. They were bursting with pride. By the time she walked off the Opry stage, tears had welled up in everyone's eyes—including LeAnn's.

"What a great night!" she said after coming off the stage. This is the kind of moment LeAnn lives for.

LeAnn was suddenly getting more attention than she had ever expected. While she thoroughly enjoyed everything coming her way, she found one thing difficult to handle: traveling to her many concert dates. While performing onstage was nothing new to LeAnn, she didn't particularly enjoy living her life on the road.

Like most country stars, LeAnn travels in a luxurious custom tour bus. A large group of people accompanies her—her parents, six band members, her comanager, her soundman, and her tutor. LeAnn does fly to some venues, but she'd much rather go in style on her bus, which is equipped with all the comforts of home. It has a mini-kitchen area with a stove, refrigerator, and microwave. At the front of the bus, a table and chairs face a TV, a stereo, and a VCR. Private bedrooms for LeAnn and her parents are in back.

There are also phones, a fax machine, and a big collection of LeAnn's favorite videos and CDs.

A second, identical bus was constructed for LeAnn's entourage to give everyone more space. "That way, when one person gets sick, everyone else doesn't get sick, too," says Belinda.

How does LeAnn like to spend her time on the bus? She engages in a variety of activities. She gets along great with the members of her band, saying, "They're so much fun. We either work out, play games, or watch movies. I recently saw the movie *Twister* and I liked it so much, I ran it twice."

LeAnn also likes catching up on her favorite TV shows, *Beverly Hills 90210* and *Friends*. "We're going to get a dish so the guys can watch football," she says, laughing.

When LeAnn isn't chilling out between performances, she's catching up on her schoolwork. Since her tutor travels with her, LeAnn has been able to maintain good grades. Because she was able to skip two grades, she now takes courses through a correspondence program from Texas Tech University. Her mom says, "The subjects are very intense. But LeAnn is making As and Bs."

While other kids LeAnn's age might find her workload impossible to handle, she manages to juggle everything with ease. LeAnn is having the time of her life. The only downside is that she misses being home.

"I was on the road for five months," she says. "In that time I had about four days off. It seems like I'm never home anymore, and that's hard. I get homesick. You don't realize how much you miss until you're away for a long time."

On the road, there's a lot of work to be done. Belinda finds that one major problem is all the laundry that needs to be done. "We don't have a washer or dryer on the bus, so the clothes just pile up," she says. "We have to wait to get to a hotel to send it out. It's a new way of learning how to live."

Belinda looks on the bright side by remembering a story she read about country superstar Loretta Lynn's early years in the business. "I heard a story that when Loretta Lynn and her husband went from radio station to radio station, she only had one dress," says Belinda. "She would wash it out between visits and hold it out the car window to dry. Now if *she* could do that, surely we'll make it through this!"

There's no doubt that living life on a moving bus can take its toll on someone as young as LeAnn. There are times when she feels extremely tired. After a long day of nonstop traveling and performing, LeAnn is usually asleep before her head hits the pillow. Because some of her shows take place at night, she has had to learn to sleep in the daytime. "There are times you don't know what day it is," she says.

LeAnn doesn't particularly like living on the road, but she does enjoy seeing different states and countries and getting up onstage to perform her music for her fans. According to Belinda, "Some of the time, when I really feel tired, I think 'Can I go on from here?' Then LeAnn gets on that stage, and the people start going crazy. You think, 'She's having a good time. She's enjoying every minute of it.' "

Sometimes LeAnn can't believe she's been given the opportunity to perform her music live. "This is what I've always wanted to do," she says, beaming. "I'm just thankful to everyone for letting me do it. This is so much fun. I wouldn't trade it for anything!"

9

LeAnn the Video Star

In the fast-paced music business, performers must be prepared to show their talents not only in recording, but also in performing live and in making videos. LeAnn has accomplished all three, but says she looked forward most to stepping in front of a camera to make her first video.

Just the way she does everything else, LeAnn dove into the taping with boundless enthusiasm. "I was real excited to make the video for 'Blue,' she says. "I've been watching everyone else's videos on CMT (Country Music Television) and TNN (The Nashville Network) for years. I couldn't believe I was actually doing my own."

Music videos serve as an extra promotion for an artist's album. The only problem is that these three- or four-minute music clips are not cheap to make. The video version of "Blue" may have helped to sell the single, but it cost Curb Records thousands of dollars to produce. In the highly competitive world of music, the price of taping a video of an artist's song has skyrocketed. Today the money being spent is between $30,000 and $200,000, with the average cost at about $75,000. Curb Records believed the expense was worth it and put the word out early that the video of "Blue" was about to be released.

After LeAnn's success with the song "Blue," music channels anxiously waited to air the video version of the most talked-about song of the year. Shot in Austin, not far from LeAnn's home, it was directed by Chris Rogers and produced by Hunter Hodge for the production company Pecos Films.

In the video, LeAnn is shown in several different shots. It begins with her singing "Blue" in a recording studio. Then it cuts to LeAnn lounging poolside, and flirting with boys. The one memorable shot is LeAnn wearing white cat's-eye sunglasses and floating lazily on a raft in Austin's famous Barton Springs.

LeAnn's videos have been praised for their polished look. She says one of the most frequent questions she's asked is where the video ideas come from. "It's a group of us who come up with the ideas," she explains. She works closely with director Chris Rogers and is involved in every aspect of the making of her videos, from the idea to the final cut.

LeAnn and Chris, who have the highest regard for each other, make a dynamite working team. When it came time to hire a director for LeAnn's second video, Chris was LeAnn's first and only choice for the job. "Chris and I have good chemistry," says LeAnn. "He always has some great ideas. I trust him very much."

After "Blue," LeAnn was on a video roll. She immediately began thinking of what she wanted to do visually with her song "One Way Ticket (Because I Can)." It was a completely different song from "Blue." She and Chris talked about it, and he came up with the idea of showing a lighter side of LeAnn.

Curb Records general manager, Dennis Hannon, agreed that this was the best way to go with LeAnn's second video. Legions of young fans who had once listened primarily to pop and rock music were buying more country records than ever before. Dennis Hannon explains that Curb Records wanted to present a new image for LeAnn in the "One Way Ticket" video. "With 'One Way Ticket,' we geared the video for a younger audience," he says.

LeAnn says, "Kids used to think country music was not cool. But there have been so many young country artists recording songs kids can relate to.

The lyrics in country songs have changed. Now it's fun and really neat music. I think that's why more kids are getting into country."

If anything shows off LeAnn's real personality, it's "One Way Ticket." Here we see LeAnn dancing, singing, and behaving like the carefree teenager she is. Trish Townsend, who is responsible for dressing most of the country stars in Nashville, provided LeAnn's wardrobe for the video. Trish usually finds clothes that fit an artist's personality. For LeAnn, she kept the style young, trendy, and chic.

"One Way Ticket" was shot in San Francisco. It was directed by Chris Rogers and produced by Jamie Amos for the production company Cloudland Filmworks. LeAnn had a great time during the taping because it gave her a chance to see the sights of San Francisco. The video was shot in several locations in and around the city. In the video, LeAnn sings her hit song standing on top of a trolley car overlooking the streets of San Francisco. She's seen shopping with friends and singing on the pier by the Oakland Bridge. "One Way Ticket" is also a fashion show; LeAnn turns up in a number of fun, hip outfits.

It's apparent how much LeAnn enjoyed working on her videos, and she looks forward to doing more. While some performers choose to tell a story in their videos, this has never mattered to LeAnn. More important to her is a good performance. In both "Blue" and "One Way Ticket," she is exceptional. Not only does she have a one-in-a-million talent, but she also has a million-dollar screen presence. She's more than an ordinary one-dimensional star. She possesses a quality that makes audiences want to see more of her.

Whenever her videos pop up on music channels, they brighten up the screen. "Blue" and "One Way Ticket" are big favorites and permanent fixtures on music channels around the country. One writer said of LeAnn's videos, "LeAnn Rimes appeals to everyone. No one can deny that she has a tremendous voice and plenty of style. She appeals to every kind of music fan. This kind of performer comes once in a generation."

When Country Music Television (CMT), the Nashville-based video music channel seen in fifty-nine countries, named the top ten videos of 1996, LeAnn's "Blue" came in at number four. LeAnn won the CMT 1996 Special Award for Female Rising Video Star of the Year. And during the week of January 13, 1997, "One Way Ticket" hit number one on CMT's Top 20 Video Countdown Chart.

The widespread appeal of her videos placed LeAnn Rimes securely in the spotlight. Inside of a year, she achieved many of her goals. Not only did she score big with her debut album, but she was also gaining attention with her slick videos. LeAnn was definitely on a blue streak of success.

10

Blazing Her Own Trail

It was one of the biggest nights in LeAnn's life. The Country Music Association Awards (CMA) invited LeAnn to participate in two segments of the show. She was scheduled to open the show with "Blue" and perform "I Want to Be a Cowboy's Sweetheart" in memory of Patsy Montana, who had died in May 1996. The pioneer singing cowgirl was being inducted into the Country Music Hall of Fame. Producers of the show thought it would be great if country's newest female star paid tribute to Patsy Montana. LeAnn was truly honored.

Not only that, but she was also nominated for two awards: Song of the Year for "Blue" and the Horizon Award for Best New Artist. *The*

Nashville Banner wrote about LeAnn's nominations, "LeAnn Rimes is a bit of a surprise, propelled by two nominations on the basis of one single."

LeAnn herself said that being nominated was "the biggest highlight of my life. This is what I've dreamed about since I was a little girl sitting in front of the TV watching Reba win awards."

LeAnn was the youngest artist ever to be nominated for a CMA Horizon Award. "It's the biggest surprise in my life," she said in one interview. "I really didn't expect it because this is my first year in the business. To think that the people in the business think so highly of me and my music is really an honor. I'll be at the show with bells on."

And she was. On the night of the thirtieth annual CMA Awards, October 2, 1996, in Nashville's Grand Ole Opry House, LeAnn drew the most attention. The star-studded event was telecast live nationwide by CBS, with an estimated eighty countries tuning in. Over the years, the CMA Awards have become a glamorous affair. The show is country music's version of the Grammys, Oscars, and Emmys. All of country music's luminaries turn out for the gala event. More than forty-four hundred attended that night.

It was LeAnn Rimes who got the show off to a great start by opening it with "Blue." Host Vince

Gill introduced her by saying, "Here's the bright future of our country music, Miss LeAnn Rimes."

She was dressed in a beautiful blue ball gown with black trim. She was performing in front of the biggest stars in country music but she wasn't a bit nervous. She remained calm, cool, and confident as she sang the song that had started her career. On the giant screen behind her were photos of her early years as a child performer.

As the audience applauded LeAnn's opening number, she walked down the steps of the stage and went to sit next to her father. Vince Gill called her back up to the stage and said a few words to the excited young singer. "That was so good. You host the show," said Vince to a laughing LeAnn.

For her next appearance on the show, she changed into a sparkling blue pants outfit and put her hair up. She came out singing Patsy Montana's song and held up the plaque that inducted the legendary singer into the Country Music Hall of Fame. LeAnn announced the induction with Marty Stuart.

LeAnn was on such a high she didn't even care that she didn't take home an award. The CMA Awards show was the first of many extraordinary nights.

She was now fully in the public eye. Articles about her rise to stardom started springing up in countless magazines and newspapers. As music's latest teen phenomenon, she was compared to teen sensations of the past. Many called LeAnn the new Brenda Lee or Tanya Tucker. The comparison was obvious, since all three singers were thirteen when they began their red-hot careers.

Brenda Lee had her first country hit at the age of thirteen, with 1957's "One Step at a Time." She went on to become one of the biggest stars of the 1950s and 1960s with songs like "Rockin' Around the Christmas Tree" and "I'm Sorry."

Brenda has a lot of praise for LeAnn. "Her voice is phenomenal on 'Blue,' " Brenda says. "LeAnn certainly doesn't sound like she's thirteen. When they gave her age on the radio, my jaw dropped." When Brenda was asked to name her favorite albums of 1996, LeAnn's CD topped her list.

In interviews Brenda Lee and Tanya Tucker were asked what they thought of the new kid in country music. They were both quick to answer and give LeAnn advice. Having already traveled down the path LeAnn was just taking her first steps on, Brenda said to one reporter, "The first thing I would tell her is to finish her education, especially high school. Don't let anything stand in the way of that. College is a plus if you can do it, but it's important to be with kids your own age and experience the things you would experience if you weren't singing and having some success and all that *that* brings.

"I think LeAnn has a big future if she can stand the rigors of all this, keep her sanity a little bit, and not be pulled by this one and that one. If people around her treat her as a person and not a product, I think she'll be fine."

Tanya Tucker was also eager to talk about LeAnn. Tanya gained fame at age thirteen when her single "Delta Dawn" hit the top ten in 1972. Since that time, she's recorded twenty-nine albums, has won many awards, and is still churning out hit records twenty-five years later.

Tanya claims she was "amazed it's taken this long for someone else to make this kind of debut. LeAnn is a good singer and I'm happy for her success. It's been a long time since we've heard a Patsy Cline influence. I think it's great that LeAnn has that feel to her voice."

LeAnn is flattered to be compared with Brenda and Tanya, but she admits, "The only real comparison is the fact that we started our recording careers when we were young." Like Brenda Lee, Tanya Tucker, and other teen superstars, LeAnn Rimes is now blazing her own trail in country music.

Someday, when people look back on the biggest teen phenomena of our times, Brenda Lee's and Tanya Tucker's names will, no doubt, still be mentioned. But by then LeAnn's name is sure to have been added to that select group of young performers who have an abundance of talent and prove their success by bursting from obscurity into superstardom. As one of the hottest names in music, LeAnn Rimes couldn't wish for anything more than she's already received!

11

A Regular Teenager

LeAnn is busier than ever and rarely has a moment to herself these days. Most of her time is devoted to her career. She loves to work, but her time off is equally important.

When LeAnn steps out of the glare of the spotlight, she craves a quiet, casual lifestyle free from worries. Her mother says, "LeAnn has always been focused on what she wants to do with her music. But when she's not performing, she's a normal Texas teenager."

One of LeAnn's favorite things to do when she has some free time is go to the mall. There's no doubt about it: LeAnn loves to shop, especially for clothes, makeup, jewelry, and hats. Her good fashion sense has influenced many girls. She has become a trendsetter by simply being herself.

Take, for example, her hairstyles, which LeAnn is always experimenting with. Her favorite way to wear her long blond hair is falling softly over her shoulders, with wispy bangs. For a different look, she uses a curling iron and hair spray.

As for makeup, LeAnn doesn't wear too much; she likes to maintain a natural look. According to her, looking natural doesn't mean not wearing any makeup at all; the trick is to apply it so that no one can tell you have any on. She uses a light foundation, a dash of brown eyeliner, blush, and pale pink lipstick.

What's the secret behind LeAnn's look? She admits she doesn't follow any strict beauty plan. She just tries to get plenty of exercise, lots of fresh air, and adequate rest. She has always been a sports enthusiast and loves getting outdoors to play softball or baseball. When she's back home in Texas and has a day to call her own, she loves to ride cutting horses (nimble horses trained to separate a cow from the herd). Her mother says, "She gets that competitive spirit from her daddy. From me, she gets the more mellow aspects of her nature."

Because she's always on the go, LeAnn can eat whatever she wants without worrying about gaining weight. What are her favorite foods? She lists Cheez-It crackers and a strawberry ice cream soda as her favorite snacks. Pasta, pizza, and steak rate high.

When it comes to clothes, LeAnn likes dressing up for events like award shows but is most comfortable wearing jeans and cropped shirts. As for shoes, she prefers flats and tennis shoes but says, "I do like wearing cowboy boots and a shoe with a low heel."

LeAnn likes to use accessories to jazz up an outfit: a hat or a cool pair of sunglasses. She often wears bracelets and rings and likes a pretty pair of earrings. Though she owns some serious jewelry, she says less expensive bracelets and earrings can be just as stylish.

As one of the best-dressed stars on the scene today, LeAnn always looks great whether she's wearing jeans and a T-shirt or a designer dress. Her secret ingredient for style is originality. "A lot of kids try to fit in with a crowd," she says. "The main thing is to set your own style. Eventually, the crowd you wanted to look like will want to look like you."

LeAnn often receives letters from other teenage girls who ask her about how important looks are in the music business. "Looks count in the music business because it helps to sell you," she says. "But looks aren't always everything. You have to see what's inside a person."

What is LeAnn really like offstage and away from show business? She describes herself as "determined and a perfectionist." When she's asked what she likes best about herself, her answer is succinct: "I don't give up!" What does she like least about herself? "I hate losing."

The private LeAnn is a bundle of energy—always in motion, totally natural, and showering everyone with her love for living. At times she makes others a little breathless; they wonder where she gets her energy. Still, people close to her have described her as gentle, kind, loving, and sensitive. "People tell me this child has an old soul," Belinda Rimes says. "She's a really good kid. It's a scary time for her. She's entering her teenage years and the life she's leading is not normal. I worry what lies ahead."

LeAnn doesn't worry because she's doing the thing she loves best. Does she feel as if she missed out on a regular childhood? "No," she answers sincerely. "A lot of people say I've missed out on things, but I don't think I have." There's no denying that LeAnn leads a very different life from other kids her age, but she's used to it. "There's not a day that's gone by in the past year that I haven't been doing something," she says. "But I've been doing this since I was five, so it's never been a really typical life. This is the way I've grown up, and I've never missed out on anything.

"I've grown up in an adult world. A lot of my friends are between twenty and eighty years old.

Some of them are in the business, and some aren't. I've always gotten along with people older than me. My closest friends are the members of my band. They've played with me on and off since I was seven, so we're real close."

LeAnn says she relates better to her older friends than to people her own age. But there have been times when she's been surprised by the antics of her older friends. "We were at a bowling alley, and one night we had a birthday cake fight," she says. "Everybody was smearing it all over each other's face. It was really funny. We had a great time. But I've never had a food fight before in my life. My forty-year-old friends were starting a food fight, and it was, like, 'Oh, my goodness.' "

Does LeAnn mind that she'll miss that important teenage experience, going to the prom? "No, I really don't," she insists. "I knew there were things I was going to have to give up. I don't mind missing the prom because I've always wanted to sing and I'm lucky to be getting the chance to do it. This is what I've grown up doing, this is what I know, and this is what's normal to me."

Many teenagers have written to LeAnn to ask her advice on dating. Although LeAnn has gone out with boys as friends, she hasn't been on a real date yet. The main reason is that she just doesn't have the time. "My schedule is too hectic," she explains. "I'm going to have to wait until things slow down a little.

"I've had boyfriends in school that I went to the movies with. But right now, I haven't had the chance to meet anybody. What's the use? I'm not in one place long enough."

LeAnn may not have time to date, but she has a definite idea of the kind of guy she likes. "Someone who is smart, honest, and has a great sense of humor," she begins. She is instantly attracted to someone who makes her laugh and is easy to talk to. "Personality is more important than looks," she says. "I like a boy who likes to have fun."

LeAnn says her dream date would be "going out to dinner and then walking along the beach . . . if I can find a beach."

She's still too young to think about dating anyone steadily or getting married, but she says there are times when she thinks about how great it would be to find someone special to share her life with. When she envisions her future, she plans to have her own family just like the happy one she grew up in. "I'm not really looking for anyone yet, but that's a part of my life I'm looking forward to," she says.

LeAnn has plenty of close friends. It's hard to keep in touch with friends at home while she's traveling, but she does her best. She sent her best friend a birthday card and told her she would call when she got home. The big problem right now is that LeAnn is rarely home. When she does get back to Texas, she usually calls her friends and they all go out to the movies.

As LeAnn's popularity has grown, she's noticed that more people recognize her. "I went to Kmart to buy toothpaste and people were staring. I heard someone say, 'I swear to you it's her,' and I thought to myself, 'Yes, it's me, buying my toothpaste!' "

LeAnn rarely goes out now without being asked to sign autographs for fans. In 1996, during Fan Fair, she had to sneak into a Nashville Burger King in disguise just to get a quick bite to eat. When fans recognized her through the disguise, she happily signed her name and posed for photos. "I really don't mind being recognized," she admits, smiling. "It's actually kind of neat. When they stop recognizing me, it's time to worry."

Asked what she likes to do with her free time, LeAnn says, "I haven't had *any* free time for about a year now. I used to, and I miss that a little, but hopefully next year I will be able to take a vacation where I could just sit and not do anything." The beach is at the top of her list of vacation spots. She adds, "I'd like to go to Denver and learn to ski. I've never done it before. I think I would *love* skiing."

In quiet times, LeAnn likes to shake off the pressures of the day by listening to the music of her favorite singers: Barbra Streisand, Patsy Cline, and Reba McEntire. LeAnn has a very large CD collection that she is constantly adding to. Not surprisingly a big country music fan, she loves the music of Alan Jackson, Bryan White, Wynonna, and the legendary Hank Williams, Sr.

Fans around the globe have started collecting photos of LeAnn, and she herself collects photos and posters. Back home in Texas, her bedroom walls are plastered with posters of Bryan White, Billy Dean, and Shania Twain. She also has tons of photos that chronicle her career and help her remember all the people she's met along the way. Among them are country stars Faith Hill, Martina McBride, David Lee Murphy, and Ty England.

LeAnn's favorite time of year is Christmas because it's a time to spend with family and friends. Christmas has always been special for the Rimeses. They love to decorate and always have a real tree with a lot of tinsel, lights, and ornaments.

In 1996, however, it didn't look as if the Rimes family would get home for the holidays. In one interview LeAnn said, "I think this year we'll be spending Thanksgiving in McDonald's." She was booked solid with concert dates all through November and December.

Traveling around the country in changing weather had a serious effect on her. In late

November she came down with a stomach virus and a mild case of bronchitis that laid her up for a couple of weeks. Trouper that she is, she tried to go on with her concerts because she didn't want to disappoint her fans. But she just couldn't go on and had to cancel several concert dates.

She went home for a much-needed break. She didn't do interviews or think about business. She just stayed in bed until she was strong enough to get back on the road.

So many things were happening! She was invited to ride on the Target stores float in the Hollywood Christmas Parade. She was also scheduled to appear on *The Tonight Show* and didn't want to cancel. Luckily, by the time the dates rolled around, she was feeling much better and traveled to California for both appearances.

She told Jay Leno, "I had about a hundred-and-three-degree fever and we had to cancel concerts, which I was sad about, but that was the worst thing. I'm just lucky I didn't get sick before this."

She also recorded a Christmas song called "Put a Little Holiday in Your Heart" that was released on a CD single with her version of "Unchained Melody." The bonus CD was exclusive to Target and sold as a dual package with LeAnn's *Blue* album.

LeAnn was all over television at Christmas 1996. She was chosen as the season's holiday spokesperson for Target stores and made a commercial in which she was surrounded by Warner Brothers animated characters. Using the same computer animation as the hit film *Space Jam* with Michael Jordan, LeAnn's commercial began as her tour bus pulled up to a country inn. LeAnn stepped out and walked toward a microphone. As she started to sing, Bugs Bunny and all the Looney Tunes began line-dancing. With Tweety Bird sitting on her shoulder, LeAnn performed her holiday song, then joined the characters on the dance floor.

"It was a lot of fun to shoot, but even more fun to watch the finished product," LeAnn says. "I was in a room by myself to do my part. All the characters were put in later."

LeAnn was also invited to take part in the CBS special *Opryland Country Christmas*, which was recorded at the Opry House in Nashville and aired on December 14. LeAnn's first reaction when she was asked to appear was, "It feels great to be included in this Christmas special. So many artists that I've looked up to for so long are on the show. To be included in this Christmas special is a very nice honor. It's always been a part of my holiday routine to watch Christmas specials with my favorite stars, and now I'm going to be on one of them, which is really neat."

LeAnn's zest for life, clean-cut image, and

determination to succeed have many of her fans looking up to her. LeAnn has a fun-loving streak, but she takes the responsibility of being a role model seriously. She maintains a strict moral code and likes to speak out to kids about the dangers of taking drugs and smoking. She is proud to set a good example for young people. "I think it's great to be thought of as a role model," she says. "A lot of parents and a lot of kids tell me they're really glad I'm a role model. I'm glad I can be a good, positive one."

Somehow, LeAnn finds time for numerous charities. Recently she went to the St. Jude's Children's Research Hospital in Memphis to visit terminally ill children. "I got to see all these little kids who are cancer patients," she says. "These children were so remarkable, so kind, and so intelligent. I mean, even these little four-year-olds would come up to you, talk to you, and be so outgoing. If I had one wish for anyone, it would definitely be for them, that a cure for cancer is found. These kids put life into perspective for everybody."

The most difficult thing for LeAnn now is to keep from spreading herself too thin. Her enthusiasm for performing, songwriting, and recording keeps her days and nights full. She hardly has time to think about everything that's happening to her. Every once in a while, she likes to get away from it all and go off to do something relaxing. Whether it's shopping, playing baseball, or riding horses, one thing is certain: When LeAnn returns to work, she's revived and ready to take on with gusto whatever her snowballing career has in store for her.

12

Runaway Success

For LeAnn, 1997 began with a bang. The first month of the year found LeAnn's name constantly in the headlines. *People* magazine, in its 1996 year-end issue, had named LeAnn one of the year's breakthrough stars. In *Rolling Stone*'s annual readers' poll, LeAnn was voted the second-favorite country artist of the year, after Johnny Cash. She was nominated for Best New Artist from *Performance* magazine, four Grammy Award nominations, and an American Music Award for Best New Country Artist. LeAnn was thrilled by it all, but the Grammys were the biggest surprise.

"I was told the night before that by eight

o'clock the next morning, the Grammy nominations would be announced," she says. "I wasn't really expecting anything. I thought maybe one, but nothing more. The next morning, my dad came in and said, 'Wake up, LeAnn, you've been nominated for four Grammys.' I just couldn't believe it."

LeAnn also learned that *Blue* was certified double platinum in Australia and that she'd been named the country's top-selling female country singer of all time. On January 10, 1997, LeAnn and her parents flew to Australia to receive her plaque and promote a sixteen-day concert tour she would be starting in March. "I took a fourteen-hour flight over from L.A. to Australia," LeAnn says. "I didn't really enjoy being on the plane for that long, but once I got to Australia, it was definitely worth the wait."

LeAnn arrived during Australia's summer and had a blast spending time in the hot sunshine in the middle of January. It was the first time she had ventured outside the United States, and she thought Australia was beautiful. "It reminds me a lot of San Francisco," she says. When the tickets for her concerts in Australia went on sale, they were sold out in a matter of hours.

In just one year, LeAnn Rimes has made a huge impact in the entertainment world. She realizes she hit the top quickly and must continue to work hard to remain there. Her primary concern now is her new album, which she is diligently working on. Before this new album hits the stores, Curb Records is releasing *LeAnn Rimes: Unchained Melody/The Early Years*. It includes seven songs from LeAnn's independent album, recorded when she was eleven, and three more songs she recorded at age twelve, including her hit single "Unchained Melody" and the first song she ever wrote, "Share My Love." It should keep LeAnn's fans happy as they wait for her follow-up to *Blue*.

So far, LeAnn has announced that her new album "will have some traditional and contemporary country. It will have a lot of me on it. My main thing is to keep recording the best music I can for everybody."

LeAnn is living the fantasy life millions might only dream of, a life of success, talent, and recognition. She is basking in the limelight but is careful to retain the fresh appeal and solid values her loving parents have taught her. The fame and fortune that have come LeAnn's way haven't spoiled her at all. She possesses great self-esteem and has remained levelheaded. For LeAnn, superstardom is a relatively new phenomenon. It's something she still can't quite grasp and probably never will.

The future of LeAnn Rimes could become one of the most interesting and exciting of all show business stories. LeAnn has been so successful with *Blue* that she can pretty much try her hand at anything. At fourteen, she has accomplished things most adults can never hope to. She looks forward to the future and dreams of all the things she still wants to achieve. She is determined to spread her creative wings and soar in many different directions—but she means to watch where she's going.

"I'm taking it day by day, to see how it goes. I don't want to rush into anything. I'm hoping my career lasts a long time," she says, then adds, "I want to continue singing and writing songs. I'd love to give acting a try. College is also an option for me. I've always wanted to help children, and I've thought about studying speech pathology."

There's no doubt that LeAnn would be successful at anything she attempted, but for now, music remains most important to her. Industry insiders have asserted that LeAnn is responsible for bringing new fans to country music. Many of her colleagues see a big future for her.

Frank Myers, of the country duo Baker & Myers, says, "LeAnn Rimes is one of the most incredible singers to come along in this century. I think she's going to leave a huge mark on the whole industry."

Dene Hallam, the program director of KKBQ radio in Houston, announces, "I think it's a safe bet to say that LeAnn Rimes will be a superstar. She has uncommon maturity for someone so young. We had her on as a guest deejay and she was one of the best we've ever had.

"The fact that she's a teenager sets her apart from the crowd. But once your attention is focused on her, you realize that there's a lot of talent there. The fact that she's fourteen years old is basically irrelevant."

That's exactly the image LeAnn wants to project. Although she's very young, she doesn't want her age to affect her career. "It definitely has helped me being a 'thirteen-year-old singing sensation,' " she says. "But I want people to know me for my music, not for my age. The age is going to go away. I won't be a teenager forever."

LeAnn says the country artist she admires most is Reba McEntire. "If I had to model my career after anyone it would have to be Reba. She's made some great business decisions in her career to stay around for twenty years, and my biggest goal right now is to stay around for a long time."

Unlike some stars who skyrocket to fame one year and disappear the next, LeAnn hopes to be singing her songs for the next "twenty or thirty years." It's obvious this sweet songbird is headed in the right direction as she climbs higher up the ladder of success. "Music is everything to me," she says.

LeAnn will be spending most of 1997 on the road, opening for Alan Jackson. "I haven't met him yet, but I've been listening to his records forever," she says. "It's going to be fun doing shows with Alan."

Poised, bright, and sophisticated, LeAnn is riding high on a wave of success, and the future holds endless possibilities for her. Being one of the music industry's hottest new talents is just the beginning for her. Success wasn't handed to her on a silver platter; she has worked hard to reach her goals, and she has a burning desire to keep her career going. She's clearly loving every minute of her success and remains passionate about her hopes, plans, and dreams.

LeAnn continues to outsell everyone on the country charts and is selling just as well on the pop charts. She has knocked down the fence that divided country music from pop. As *Blue* continued its reign as the number one country album in America, it climbed back into fourth place on *Billboard's* pop album chart the week of January 13, 1997, passing such top sellers as Alanis Morrissette, Bush, and Toni Braxton. For the first time since the days of Garth Brooks, country is once again at the forefront of American music, and the girl responsible for it all is a bubbly, talented fourteen-year-old from Texas named LeAnn Rimes.

Country's sweetheart has nothing to be blue about these days. She has paved the way for country's new sound by returning to its traditions. In doing so, she has revitalized country music for a younger generation. A true star with a long career ahead of her, LeAnn promises to keep taking chances and coming up with surprises.

Perhaps her biggest surprise was the night of the 39th Annual Grammy Awards. LeAnn, dressed in a long, light blue dress, looked stunning the night of the awards, held at Madison Square Garden in New York. Out of her four nominations, she won for Best Female Country Vocal and Best New Artist. Songwriter Bill Mack received the Best Country Song Grammy for LeAnn's hit "Blue."

Named Best New Artist, she walked up the stairs to the microphone. "I never expected this at all," she said, clutching the Grammy. "This award means more to me than anything in the world!" At just fourteen years old, LeAnn Rimes entered the Grammy history books. Watch her success!

LeAnn's Fact File

Real name: LeAnn Rimes
Birthdate: August 28, 1982
Birthplace: Jackson, Mississippi
Height: 5′5″
Weight: 115 pounds
Hair color: Blond
Eye color: Blue
Parents: Wilbur and Belinda Rimes
Pet: A dog named Sandy
Current residence: Garland, Texas
Astrological sign: Virgo
First ambition: To be a singer
Favorite sports: Softball, baseball
Favorite color: Blue

Favorite foods: Pasta, pizza, chicken, steak and potatoes

Favorite sandwich: Grilled ham and cheese on white bread

Favorite dessert: Strawberry ice cream soda

Favorite midnight snack: Cheez-It crackers

Favorite actors: Kevin Costner, Morgan Freeman

Favorite actress: Whoopi Goldberg

Favorite movies: *The Shawshank Redemption*, *Twister*

Favorite TV shows: *Friends*, *Beverly Hills 90210*

Favorite female singers: Patsy Cline, Reba McEntire, Whitney Houston, Barbra Streisand, Wynonna

Favorite male singers: Hank Williams, Sr., Alan Jackson, Bryan White, Billy Dean

Favorite pastime: "I love to go shopping. That's a girl thing."

Favorite hobbies: Riding, tennis, swimming

Favorite nail polish colors: Pink, purple

Favorite clothes: T-shirt and jeans, anything comfortable

Favorite school subject: Math

Least favorite school subject: Science

Most exciting moment: Meeting President Clinton. In December 1996, LeAnn was invited to flip the switch at the annual tree lighting ceremony at the White House. Afterward, she and her parents met President Clinton and First Lady Hillary Rodham Clinton.

Professional ambition: To keep singing for twenty or thirty years

Worst thing she's ever tasted: An anchovy

Little-known fact: She used to dot the *i* in *Rimes* with a circle.

Pet peeves: "None yet!"

Ideal guy: Nice, caring, with a good personality

Dream date: Dinner and a walk on the beach

Where to write to LeAnn:

LeAnn Rimes Fan Club
Belinda Rimes, President
Twin Sixties Towers, Suite 816
6060 North Central Expressway
Dallas, TX 75206

LeAnn Rimes
c/o Curb Records
47 Music Square East
Nashville, TN 37203

LeAnn's Thoughts

On Her Success

"They're calling me a fourteen-year-old sensation. I just hope someday they call me a twenty-one-year-old sensation."

On Traditional Country Music

"I think it's important for my generation to learn where the roots of country are."

On Coping with Fame

"It hasn't changed me. But if it has, I hope it's been for the better. The only major difference is that people recognize me when I go out."

On How She Likes to Dress

"I dress all different ways. It depends on how I feel.

Some days, I will just wear jeans and cropped shirts. Other days, I'll wear something totally different."

On School

"I'm much happier being tutored because I feel like I'm getting a better education. I don't think I'm missing out on anything by not going to a regular school."

On Peer Pressure

"I think that when anyone gives in to peer pressure, it's because they don't feel good about themselves. But that's not a problem for me because I always try to feel good about myself."

On Achieving Goals

"If you have a dream or goal, don't stop until you reach it. If you really want to accomplish something, don't let anyone stand in your way. If you truly want to achieve something, then go for it."

On Being an Only Child

"I think it helps being an only child in the business I am in. My parents get to spend lots of time with me. My father is my producer and comanager and my mom helps out with everything and they both travel with me, so it works out really well. Now that I'm older, I would like to have a brother or sister."

On Patsy Cline
"Patsy Cline has been a big influence on me. I love her music. Just before I recorded 'Blue,' I had a dream about Patsy Cline. I could see her face, and she told me she couldn't record 'Blue' and wanted me to do it. It was pretty cool. It made me feel as if I had her blessing."

On Stage Fright
"I never have stage fright. I credit that to starting as young as I did. I've been onstage since age five. Being onstage and meeting new people all the time helped me get past my shyness."

On Changing Her Life
"Things have gone so well. I don't think there is anything I could change that would make it any better right now."

On Her Success with Her Song "Blue"
" 'Blue' is a big part of my success. It was my first song. It was the first song everybody heard. 'Blue' was totally different from what everyone had out. It was the traditional country. I think if I came out with anything else, I wouldn't have the success I have now. I credit a lot of my success to 'Blue.' "

Discography

LeAnn Rimes—All That
(Nor Va Jak, released 1994)
LeAnn's independent album. Includes the original versions of "Blue" and "I'll Get Even with You."

LeAnn Rimes—Blue
(MCG/Curb, released July 1996)

Tracks

"Blue"
Written by Bill Mack

"Hurt Me"
Written by Deborah Allen, Rafe VanHoy, and Bobby Braddock

"One Way Ticket (Because I Can)"
Written by Jody Rodman and Keith Hinton

"My Baby"
Written by Deborah Allen

"Honestly"
Written by Christi Dannemiller and Joe Johnston

"The Light in Your Eyes"
Written by Dan Tyler

"Talk to Me"
Written by LeAnn Rimes, Ron Grimes, and Jon Rutherford

"I'll Get Even with You"
Written by Coweta House

"Cattle Call" (Duet with Eddy Arnold)
Written by Tex Owens

"Good Lookin' Man"
Written by Joyce Harrison

"Fade to Blue"
Written by Anne Reeves, Jim Allison, and Lang Scott

LeAnn Rimes—Put a Little Holiday in Your Heart
(Curb Records, released December 1996)

Bonus CD with two tracks:

"Put a Little Holiday in Your Heart"
Written by Roger Wojahn, Scott Wojahn, and Greg Wojahn

"Unchained Melody"
Written by Alex North and Hy Zaret

LeAnn Rimes—Unchained Melody/The Early Years
(Curb Records, released February 1997)

Tracks

"Cowboy's Sweetheart"
"I Will Always Love You"
"Blue Moon of Kentucky"
"River of Love"
"The Rest Is History"
"Broken Wing"
"Yesterday"
"Sure Thing"
"Share My Love"
"Unchained Melody"

Videography

Music Videos

Blue
Directed by: Chris Rogers
Produced by: Hunter Hodge
Production company: Pecos Films
Time: 2:47
Filmed in: Austin
Released: May 30, 1996

One Way Ticket (Because I Can)
Directed by: Chris Rogers
Produced by: Jamie Amos
Production company: Cloudland Filmworks
Time: 3:42
Filmed in: San Francisco
Released: September 18, 1996

About the Author

Grace Catalano is the author of two *New York Times* best-sellers: *New Kids on the Block* and *New Kids on the Block Scrapbook.* Her other books include biographies of Leonardo DiCaprio, Brad Pitt, Joey Lawrence, Jason Priestley, Paula Abdul, Gloria Estefan, Richard Grieco, Fred Savage, River Phoenix, Alyssa Milano, and Kirk Cameron. She is also the author of *Teen Star Yearbook* and *Country Music's Hottest Stars.* Grace Catalano has edited numerous magazines, including *CountryBeat*, *Country Style*, *The Music Express*, *Star Legend*, *The Movie Times*, *Rock Legend*, and the teen magazine *Dream Guys.* She and her brother, Joseph, wrote and designed *Elvis: A Tenth Anniversary Tribute* and *Elvis and Priscilla.* Grace Catalano lives on the North Shore of Long Island.